the pace *of* our feet

by "*Quote*"

The Pace Of Our Feet © and ℗ "Quote" L.L.C.

and Great Quail Music

All songs written by "Quote"

"Quote" is Justin Tam and Jamie Bennett

Produced by Mike Odmark, Justin Tam, and Jamie Bennett

Recorded and Mixed by Mike Odmark at Big Beard Studios

Mastered by Matt Odmark

Literature Edited by Dr. Maggie Monteverde and Jadyn M. Stevens

Cover Art by Sara La and James De Boér: Cover and disc design by Emily Keafer

Book Design by Eveready Press

www.quotemusic.net

www.myspace.com/quotemusic

Printed in the USA

ISBN: 978-0-9814694-3-0

the pace *of* our feet

by "*Quote*"

EVEREADY PRESS
1817 Broadway • Nashville, Tennessee 37203
615-327-9106
www.eveready-usa.com

Foreword

The Pace of Our Feet is the fruition of an accidental idea—an unexpectedly large fish smiling back through an aimlessly cast net. An idea one would be pretentious to proclaim as unique, yet equally unwise to ignore: the idea of communicating inspiration through multiple mediums.—*The Pace of Our Feet* combines visual art and literature with music in an attempt to capture both the *eyes* and the *ears*.

The songwriters of "Quote," Jamie Bennett and Justin Tam, set out to tell a few tales, some tall, some true. Each narrative began simply, with a tune and a lyric. The sweltering summer of 2007 produced recordings of these songs with the aid of Nashville's finely tuned ears and Ireland's strings. "Quote" then recruited the trusted pens and brushes of authors and visual artists to translate their sound into ink and paint.

After a year of patient prodding and pushing, fussing and fuming, "quote" has managed to finish *The Pace of Our Feet*. So find the nearest tree or closest riverbank, stop your watch for a while, and cast an open net.

CONTENT

KEROSENE

We walked home on an avocado road in dirty groves,
Disney Lane was all we'd known.
We ran through the knee-deep leaves,
the moon was smoke, moving through the grapefruit trees.
I was hiding out in that smaller town:
everything is looking different now

Memories repeat
like kerosene lamps flickering.
Heaven knows where children go,
when all their dreams are growing old.

Wooden guns in our hands,
the sheriff runs; he can't catch the prisoner man.
Painted skies overhead,
I felt alive, when they were turning red.

lyrics by Jamie Bennett & Justin Tam

Repeat
Watercolor, Ink, and Colored Pencil on Paper
2008
22 x 30 in.
LA Bachman
Nashville, TN
www.labachman.com
la@labachman.com

KEROSENE

by Q Bennett

One half mile from Shelby Bottoms,
where the train shrills
and shakes my bed frame,
the faded gloom of the sun rests
on a light pole outside my window.

I drift, shedding the day's luster.
Mary has gone home,
likely dreaming of her garden,
sifting through a gamut of seeds.
Her charm lies latent inside my head.

Marche's customers are still squawking,
exhaling a final plume of smoke before waltzing in
to forward their questioning demands.
"I might like some Manchego,
Oh and hunny! A glass of Prosecco?"

4

The precipice of the day hangs
not on the day itself
but in this memorial rendezvous,
forever following and floating
between coherence and sleep.

Thought lingers through the week,
past months,
the year two-thousand and seven,
twiddling on a horizon
line stretched thin.

Life stares with gaping eyes
as if at a map nailed to the wall.
A wick lit with kerosene
casts a shadow upon its face
flickering between states.

I fall from its coordinates
to home,
two thousand thirty-eight miles
west of these houses that litter
east of the Cumberland River.

To Disney Lane.
My foot squelches avocado leaves,
as blood oranges boil in the afternoon sun.
A palm tree looms over our house
and my backyard trampoline,

where we spent the night on its sleek fibers,
fists clasping cheap beer,
listening to the coyotes yelp,
cool and cacophonous,
giddy over their catch of dinner.

Winds bereft of worry
touched the soft tissue in our brains,
creating memories deeply woven,
a beautiful pane
stuck to my gut.

There inside memory resides
silent, until some tiny substance
tinges the sense of a sense,
the air redolent with lilac and sage
after it rains, baptizing the earth with holy fingers.

We lay in cocoons,
older brother and I,
spinning stories and watching for space ships,
imagining what we'd do if one landed
its gigantic legs arching above our heads.

We stole the night with our juvenile mischief,
ransacked the ruddy hills
with tiny feet and cross-haired eyes,
filled our lungs deep with childish fear and adventure
till they could no longer satiate our hunger for fun.

Brother and I stood with father on our rooftop
like metal rods amidst lightning showers,
clouds red as a Mojave sand storm.
We of nine, twelve, and thirty-eight years,
our hands shook in awful wonder.

Rarely mindful of the past,
we had no future in mind,
our eyes fastened to the hour.
Life was free, lacking independence,
desire a sidestep away from fulfillment.

Thoughts become pendular,
twisted and swinging in the back of the brain;
I swoon over and over them in a sort of trance,
as the light of the kerosene lamp wanes,
and night travels to morning.

Between sleep and somber waking,
I have attained only a glimpse
into this rhythmic rolling river,
which flows outside my window,
past worn wooden tracks, and spoiled grass,

I, a somersaulting baboon,
who won't quit clapping my hands
and jumping into the crystal current,
where past and present have assembled
in my sojourning slumber.

THE CASPIAN PARADE

From the oil rocks of the Caspian,
we're drifting over the sea.
We'll chart the course on our cabin doors,
while drinking the saltiest breeze.
The taste on our lips gets better each sip,
better each sip of the day.
So don't delay; make your escape.
We're leavin', my friend,
on The Caspian Parade

The Caspian Parade
is hoistin' up the mast.
They're pullin' up the slack,
never looking back.
The Caspian Parade
is passing by your shores.
They're spying on your ports,
'cause they'll be back for more.

Divide the lake into equal stakes.
The Union thinks we should share,
but we'll fight the North on this history course,
and the Persians will join the affair.
So don't despair - we're taking our aim,
'cause this is the stand of The Caspian Parade.

lyrics by Justin Tam

Caspian Parade
Oil on Canvas
2008
52 x 72 in
Casey Pierce
Nashville, TN
www.caseypierce.com
casey@caseypierce.com

THE CASPIAN PARADE

by Frank Martino

The eastern sea stirs, and now the gulls flap
A wild beat, and a rare storm broods in the sky.
Currents of air and moisture collide, coiling
Around each other, primed, ready to flood
The sunset lands west of the Caspian Sea.
There, a man stands, facing the faded coast
Where the gulls linger in the steady winds,
Drifting on wings soiled by the shadow sand
Of beaches where the birds scavenge for food.
He suffers to breathe, in deep streams of dried air,
And another man, among twelve, fingers
A crumb of dirt into the rough dwellings
Of stick figures who mimic life lost
In the promise of oil, a crude promise of wealth.
A friend kneels nearby, seeking south, southwest.

He heats the last breath of prayer and with shins on the ground,
His arms by his side, and his head touching the caps
Of his knees, he forms a deep arch in his back
And curls into a taut bow filled to entirety
With faith that love of God will survive his death.

Three others prepare for dinner, a meal
To take their minds away from the ugly stench
Of these hills which are engulfed distant, swollen dreams
Of the eternity that encroaches on their lives,
Here or hereafter, while the war continues.
The three use what little is left after their slow parade
Came back, stumbling down from the hills to the west
Where they camp on a tall slope that wanes toward the sea.
As each man settles into an eerie silence,
One of the three of the thirteen collects his fire
From the fallen branches of parched trees and imagines
That he can hear the Caspian as its waters flow
In depression and ebb away from the shore,
Cowering into itself as it pollutes the ancient life
That relies on its swell for a place to call home
When all earth elsewhere is tainted by greed.

And as the second sets a pot to boil,
Filling it with common spice and animal fat
Slowly cooked by his wife's favorite design,
He swallows the fragrant scent of turmeric each time
And breathes in the remote memory
Of her quiet ways, exhaling the night air
Of each dinner they ate, knowing the value
Of a life lived within a loving family.
The last of the three leans over a butchered lamb
He stole from the Armenians when the sun rose,
And as he skewers it with the sharper point
Of his walking stick, he gags on the thought that he killed
No less than five men in the morning skirmish
And that he'll need to kill at least five more
To survive the month, realizing that men have more
In common with the nature of beasts than they'd admit.
And, as crabs come to shore unsure of whether
They will find a feast or a bird ready for a meal
Of its own, so all but one of the men begin
To settle down by the fire to find time stopped

By a meal, in hopes that no feast will be their last.
Yet, the passing of time is like the storm
Whose flood will be unstoppable and won't break
Under the influence of any that live.

A young man among them speaks prematurely
Of a life to begin after the battles conclude,
As if he was already victorious, like the eagle
That preys on Caspian seals, patiently stalking
The young as the mothers fatten their pups with milk,
Before wings swoop down sea-level for the kill
And ascend the dusk's sky with a bloody prize
That squirms in the stiff and deadly grip of their talons.
He gloats with a pride masked by his words of hope
While he preaches to his friend, a cousin by his uncle,
Though the cousin, barely a man, has no heart to reply
As it hasn't been long since the free hours of his days
Were spent studying prose at a school in Karabakh,
Nor has much time passed since his brother was shot

In the street and the body fell limp to the ground
As his fraternal eyes became vacant.
So when the man, barely a man, turns red
And his vision blurs in a tempered mask of sadness,
He unleashes a rage on his cousin's blatant vanity
And, though ten men surround their needless brawl,
The only man who succeeds in halting
The assault is the one who looks for the sea. Letting
His finger pull the trigger, he howls for the end
Of all wars and shoots death on an eagle.
As the bird drops to their sides, they know the dread
Of combat and how it exposes men as they are.
So now they lick their wounds with complaint,
But take each word as a grain of loose sand
And let the quarrel drift away in the winds
With the rain that can't reach these unholy thirsts
And will not fall till the sun's final set
When every man camps under stars of peace.

CASTLES

I travel alone, no matter where I go,
'cause nobody stays when you're walkin' away with a wandering soul.
I met a messenger; she was a passenger.
On a Westbound ride, she found the whites of my eyes,
through the holes in the earth.

She said, "You can't have everything. Every puppet has its strings."

San Francisco's not that far away,
but people change directions every day.
The desert sands may slip through your hands,
so build your castles while you've got the chance.

I took a sailor's name and threw out the stowaways.
The Pacific clouds seem brighter now, but I miss those darker days...

I guess you can't have everything.
Every puppet has its strings.

San Francisco's not that far away,
but people change directions every day.
The desert sands may slip through your hands,
so build your castles while you've got the chance.
You've got the Chance.
You've got the Chance.

lyrics by Justin Tam

Passenger
Acrylic, Oil, and Latex Paint on Wood
2008
54 x 38 in
Kuntal Patel
Fallbrook, CA
itskuntal@yahoo.com

LINES UNREACHABLE

by Sandy Craven

Unaware, drowning in toxins of overused air, I awake. Somewhere between Pittsburgh and Chicago—an underused stretch of land I observe, though to be fair, I have been asleep for most of it.

Reaching for something familiar, I fumble in my duffle bag, only to remember: no second-hand smoke for these my weary co-travellers—even if they'd prefer it to the stale air we've all been sharing. No, sir, can't have that.

So I find The Atlas, my sacred text for this journey. All dog-eared and wrinkled. Believe me, I've planned it all out with no intention of following through. But peruse I do anyhow, eye-tracing my bright red sharpie line indicating the required course. Lancaster to Pittsburgh, Pittsburgh to Chicago, and eventually…San Francisco. The train and tracks and sharpie line read to me in their window reflection like a play; characters cast, sets built, the plot unchanging and unnegotiable. Some people, if given the opportunity and a goal at the end, will walk a straight line for 3000 miles. Others need steel and smoke and blinding speeds to encase them to ensure their journey finds its destination. And once there, they flop about like fish on dry land, wondering why it felt so free and wonderful to sit and do nothing but dream—of traveling.

Eyes to the glass again and green, black, green, black, green swifting past. It's like all the trees and the dark separations between them are creating an endless stream of bar-codes framed in green. I try to scan the lines, like a map, or a damn dot-to-dot puzzle. I have point A to point B, and for now that will do.

The motion has me dizzy and swooning. I'm caught in the blurredscape of land and it adds to my growing nausea. Everyone, everything I pass has a purpose, a place to go.

Me, I have no aim. I have an idea, a need I suppose, but its purpose floats away before I get a glimpse of what it is. I have left the place I have known, perhaps to find it, perhaps just to keep moving.

His hand closes around my wrist with a pressure that is firm, but lacks aggression.

"What exactly are you doing with this, son?" He says "son" not like a Father would say it. His voice is colder and more removed. I am not his son, so he faces my transgression cooly, utilizing established terms of reference to a young man he does not know.

I hold a pack of baseball cards…which sounds completely ridiculous now. Delving head-on into one cliche while fully defying it. All American, my ass. Teamwork, honor, and fairness were clearly not attributes I learned from the game whose cards I loved at 10 years old. As such I was not much interested in shelling out the $5 I was required to exchange for them.

"What are you doing, son?" His voice rose in volume. I should have answered him, I know.

"I'm stealing them, sir."

The bruises on my back from my Real Father's belt lasted for two weeks, two weeks changing for gym class in the shitting stall because I didn't want my dad to go to jail.

I move uncomfortably almost expecting them to still be there. The trees keep on streaming by. Word from the conductor, or pilot, or whatever is that we will not reach Chicago for another two hours.

I know nothing about this city of Chicago, but the thought that I am headed there at blank miles an hour is exhilarating. Big City is an alluring concept. Pittsburgh is big, sure, but not like Chicago. It doesn't get mentioned in nearly as many songs.

And now I notice the Girl in the corner of the train. She is back in the end of the car, by that no-man's-land where the cars connect. Looking at her, for a moment I find myself thinking of action heroes bravely stepping between freight cars, over the rapidly-moving tracks and imminent death to catch their villain. But this is a passenger train, and I'm thrown off as I realize that despite the lack of danger, no one leaps from car to car here. We just languish in our space until the train stops and someone tells us we can step outside and smoke. Or move freely about the cabin. Or talk to mysterious girls by the luggage rack.

She is dark-haired and reading something. Impressive enough to those who suffer from motion-sickness. But she is impressive anyhow, on all accounts. Slightly built and oddly beautiful. Big nose, an unkempt appearance, a vague sense that nothing anyone says or thinks about her will matter.

I'm trying not to stare, but the attempt does not yield the projected results: She looks up and my way. And that awkward eye-contact-thing happens. I look away to hide my gaze, though we both know fully how established it already is. I study The Atlas intently for a moment, looking at but not really seeing my well-planned red line, buying time until

I can sneak another glance, and make things worse.

It's been about a minute, I assume, so I lift my eyes. And I'm startled to find hers looking right back at me. Shit. The jig is up. Has she been looking at me this whole time? This whole, full minute?

She smiles, sets down her book and speaks to me.

"Wanna come over here?" the Girl says loudly. There are other passengers around us, and several of them are startled by the sudden breach of our collective mutual agreement of silence while on the train. Now there are many, many eyes on me, and I am struck by the familiarity of this feeling. Like when you're in a store or restaurant and the call goes out that YOU have left your headlights on. Except nobody knows it's you until you get up and make the walk of shame to the parking lot to save your battery.

I decide to save my battery.

As I approach the Girl's seat at the back of the car, she slides over to the window, leaving me a place beside her. I sit down with my duffle bag on my lap and wait a moment before I turn to her. Our introductions do not go as planned.

"Do you like Faulkner?" she asks, and I glance down at the book she is reading. It isn't Faulkner.

"Um..." I'm a stammering fool and I know it. "I thought only Southerners liked Faulkner."

She chuckles. "Yeah, I guess Southerners and Northerners with identity crises."

Oh god, she had me.

"So what *are* you reading?" I ask with the emphasis on 'are,' totally giving away my inspection of her reading material.

"What's your name?" she inquires, her eyes hot branding irons.

"My name is Brendan," I reply.

This is not my real name. Though I've always liked the name, I don't know why I said it. New beginnings? Being cut loose from myself?

I had a trampoline growing up. Taunted by the oppressiveness of summer in Pennsylvania, as kids we would wait until sundown and then sit out on it, watching the fireflies send out alerts with their glowing behinds. We would bask in the waning heat, if only for a moment. Even in the twilight our skin sparkled with perspiration, the humidity tight on us like a blanket we could never shake off. But these were our hours of peace. Without the sunshine, the heat was alright. We could bear it as the sun gently faded into an all-consuming night.

My best friend was a delicate young lady, a neighbor. She didn't have a trampoline, and that is how we became acquainted. At first we would just jump for hours, playing the games kids play on trampolines, crack the egg, stuff like that. Sweat rolling down our faces and soaking our shirts, her mom would lean over the chain-link fence separating our yards and insist we drink some water before we died of heat stroke, for heaven's sake. Then day would evolve into evening, and exhausted, we would settle down to watch the stars come out and talk.

That was early middle-school. With age and higher education came the obligatory and consummate adolescent awkwardness. Of course I had felt stirrings of sexuality toward my young lady best friend from early on. But those feelings were safely relegated to personal and fleeting fantasies, to a warmth in my body as we chatted on the trampoline.

After she went home, I used to lay awake in those Pennsylvania summer nights, when temperatures never dropped below 90, even deep after sunset. The heat would ward off sleep above my father's living room, but the rotating fan on my dresser provided an illusion of rest for me. I could time my breathing by its intermittent washes of propelled air. I could almost dream.

The kids at school began to talk about the two of us doing things I was embarrassed to admit I had imagined. Much as I wanted to fit in, I denied everything, and honestly, it wasn't even to protect her honor, which was something I hadn't even begun to understand. I denied it because it was true, and I knew she would deny it too.

Now the overhead fans are whirring in a bar somewhere on W Adams St. in Chicago, and their soft sound is having its usual effect. I am half-drunk, half-asleep and completely, fully alive. Unhinged, even.

The Girl and I are sitting a few feet apart on stools, nursing some micro-brew stouts and every once in a while saying things to each other.

"Where are you going?" she ponders aloud, not exactly asking me.

"California," I reply anyway. "I'm going to be a sailor...from a port in San Francisco. It's Old School, the Old World." I don't why I said it—it was just the first thing that seemed to fit.

"Hmm." She is still looking down and into her beer, slowly swishing it in circles. "Why a sailor?"

"Sailors have adventures. They travel, they see the world. It used to be the way people learned anything new, before the internet ruined everything."

"So you're a romantic." She looks over to me now.

"Being a sailor isn't so romantic," I counter. "There's the months at sea, the seasickness, the complete absence of women." I'm grinning.

"But the isolation allows a person to truly desire something," she replies, staring down again, toying with a lighter. "You have nothing but the sea and your dreams to stimulate you. That in itself is romantic. The longing and the imagination it requires. Having something, an opportunity in front of you isn't romantic. The unavailability of that, though, is romance."

"Sounds a little defeatist." Now I'm looking down, feeling out-smarted.

"Maybe," she says, then swigs her beer, "But maybe the hope is what matters. Maybe it's the site of the horizon that really is the end of the world, maybe that's the hope that makes it romantic."

"But these days we know what is at the end of that horizon," I argue. "We can google a damn map of the world. If I was shipping off from the California coast, I'd know where I was heading. I'd be able to track it with fucking sophisticated equipment! Or...someone would."

"Then why did you say it was adventurous?" she asks calmly.

I let my eyes relax as I consider her question. They focus unintentionally on the mirror placed behind the bar, and now I can see myself staring back, alone, confused, and lost. I try to answer her in my head. 'Because the Sea is full of mystery and we don't really know what goes on down there. Because there is always the chance of being marooned on a desert island. Because...because the old maps display intricate drawings of sea monsters and part of me believes they're actually there.'

I say nothing.

"How far," she asks, "do you think you'd have to get out into the Pacific Ocean before you started to realize that no one could save you out there? How deep would the ocean have to be beneath you before it made your head swim with that possibility?"

And I am struck with questions of my own. How far would I have to be in the middle of the continent to realize that I could not feasibly walk to the ocean's shore? How long 'til I no longer looked to the specs in the constellations and the horizon, but, instead, only to a map and dotted, red lines?

Again, I say nothing.

My Father was a lawyer, highly educated and sharply focused. And mostly a nice guy.

He didn't beat us often. Certainly not enough to have us removed from his care, though honestly, I'll never really know that for sure. We never told anyone, so the cops never got involved.

But when he beat us it was hard. A belt swung with the hardware towards our bodies, a fist to our abdomen to force submission. Granted, these punishments were dealt out only for truly bad behavior: my shoplifting exploits, my sister caught in the throes with her teenage lover. Or that's how I managed to justify it as I grew older. I realized the law does not look kindly on bruises acquired by a parent's hands and chose to protect this man, this Father of mine.

And then I think I got confused. Loyalty and morality merging purple, orange, and grey in my mind as I tried, so hard, to prevent some dramatic legal battle from swirling my Father down the drain and out of our lives.

So I allowed it to continue, the beatings and the fear of beatings. Fear evolving into anger, anger into rage. Another beating. Rage to numbness, numbness to apathy.

It was a true decay: slow and smelly. First the wounds of the corpse fester until the blood stops flowing. Then a pause, and rigor mortis sets in; stiffness and stillness. Then the stench pervades as molecules that held the flesh together break down, dissolve, and release their gases, until they are gone.

Until I was gone.

Myself and the Girl are walking now, swimming a little from the drink. We know that Lake blank is around here somewhere, and it seems like a worthwhile destination for two young things caught up in the moment. But as to which direction and how far, we are ignorant. Doesn't matter, though. We are laughing and leaning on each other, stumbling along as the evening deepens.

She sees a lamppost ahead and frolics toward it, leaping up and swinging on the spire, singing a show-tune whose origin I cannot recall. I laugh until I'm sick, choking on the air and the alcohol and the thought that this will all end so soon.

And she hollers at me from her slight vantage, "What do you want!?"

"I want the promised land," I answer without thinking. I want the ocean and the sun and a future that never ends, or gets too cold or too hot. Or boring. But I only say again, "I want the promised land."

"Yooooouuu knoooow," she sings the words to me in some mangled melodic version of her show tune, "you can't have everything." And the profundity of the thought cannot even sink in before she loses her footing on the lamppost and gravity flings her body toward the street.

I grab her as she comes down, whirling around, feeling the momentum of her outstretched legs catch the air and push us along, faster, firmer. We laugh until we can see the sun.

I'm on the train again. Goodbyes long past, I'm alone. With my duffle bag and my Atlas.

The Girl failed to mention during our respite in Chicago that that was indeed her final destination. Upon returning to the train station, she extended a hand and clenched mine unexpectedly. "See ya, man" she had intoned, sort of casually, sort of seriously. Sort of over.

Up and down went our fists. The warm spring sun blinding through the windows, our faces obscured in the intensity. And then I was on the train, facing my future.

I settle down, wish for a cigarette, then pull out the Atlas and watch the red sharpie fly past my window towards California.

It's easy for me to think, as I sit among a hundred or so other people, that I am the only person with a view of the horizon as god. That place where the earth meets the sky, which is clearly visible yet does not exist. I will never reach that thick dark line, and no one else will either. Somehow, this is comforting to me. The impossibility of the goal makes failure impossible. It is ineffable. Unreachable. Perfect.

My name is Brendan, and I am going to be a sailor.

UNTIL THE SUNRISE

Look what I found now,
just messin' around.
I found the sweetest tune
under the clouds

I'll put it on for you,
spin it round and around.
I'll sing a verse or two,
sing it out loud,

'Cause I'm a desperate man
in love with the blues.
So clap your hands,
and tie your shoes.

We're gonna play all night (until the sunrise).
We're gonna turn it on now (until the sunrise).
We're gonna do this right (until the sunrise),
until the sun comes up (the sun comes up).

Who's that sittin' next to you,
wearin' that dress?
She's got the prettiest brown eyes
that I've ever met.

This is your chance, little boy,
to be a man.
I'll give you one more little line,
before I ask her to dance,

'Cause I'm a desperate man,
in love with the blues.
So clap your hands,
and tie your shoes.

lyrics by Justin Tam

Until the Sunrise
Mixed Media
2008
6 x 8.5 in - per panel
Amanda Ball
Nashville, TN
www.myspace.com/myredwagonart
ally.ball@gmail.com

BURNING BRIGHT

by Ashley Strosnider

Since I'm down on my luck, "Fill her up!"— toss one back.
There's a comfort in that, like the swing of an axe.
The alarms were loud as we blocked off the shafts,
locked friends in dead ends, stopped the blaze in its tracks.
Thick smoke went down easy with every deep breath,
coated tongues, filled the lungs of the men we had left.
But with a cough and sore hands my survival suggests
each new gasp of clean air is a criminal theft.

Every working man needs a bartender to trust,
a place to unwind, to pay up, with disgust.
Except that I know my dark layer of dust
will blend in when the shadows grow long, if I just
sit down with the others, like each normal night,
and wave for a drink like the boss and his guys—
with soft hands and straight collars, the same shade of white,
still unstained and unbothered, unready to fight.

I was born to the world buried under this town,
where the tiniest spark starts a flame underground
that a fountain of mothers' tears never could drown.
"But, hey! Tommy, boy, pass that cigarette down!"
And I'll light up a match that's as hot as my sweat,
but dirt under my nails just won't let me forget
that all my inheritance is nothing but debt.
'Cause tonight I'm alive,' there's no worse it could get.

The best song and the worst charge identical costs
and no money's clean when it clinks in the slot.
But to keep this song spinning, I'll give all I've got,
and as long as she's grinning, I'll pray she forgot.
I'd spend my whole savings to make this town dance
'til my pockets hold nothing but holes and black sand.
If that boy dancing next to her won't be quick, take his chance,
I'll walk right over there and take her by the hand.

See, it's coal in her blood that stains her dark eyes.
If I kissed her as soft as the skin on her thighs,
or sucked hard on her mouth, till that poison's refined,
could I unearth her heart buried down in that mine?
Her dress and my sorrow, deep blues to compare,
And I'd do all I could to carry her despair.
But there's no rubbing my stains off and she's lucky there;
none of my sins will get stuck in her hair.

Though she's all I could hope for as dawn creeps up fast,
everything I had yesterday's gone in a flash—
And tomorrow does nothing but echo the past;
I'll never stop hearing the sound of that blast.
But what's happened is finished and can't be undone.
I'm freed, now, I guess, owe allegiance to none,
and to some it might seem that my life's just begun.
I've got nothing to lose, burning bright as the sun.
So I'll dance like I'm happy, tell all sorts of lies,
drink and make promises, until the sunrise.

SOW AND YIELD

Quite drenched with sweat,
appearances unkempt.
Toil, parched with thirst,
face covered in dirt.
Separate the stones from the rocks,
simplify the moments and the
thoughts,
count on being fucked.

Get me out of this race.

Words kept inside,
no one to confide.
Tolerate the rage from the sun,
do what you've been told till it's done,
count on being shunned.

Get me out of this race.

I can't complain,
I'm getting paid
to raise the sons
that bear my name.
I till the fields
to sow and yield
a better day.

lyrics by Jamie Bennett & Justin Tam

Sow and Yield
Graphite, Frosted Mylar, and Paper
2008
13 x 13 in
John Whitten
Nashville, TN
www.johnpwhitten.com
johnwhitten@mac.com

SOW AND YIELD

by Motke Dapp

Stone.
Rock.

Rock.

The separation process takes days. Weeks.
Once we're finished with one field, we move to the next.

Rock.

Stone.

"Honey, come back to bed."

My wife's voice shakes me from the searing light of the field, with its hot wind, fuzzy-edged images, and echoing sounds. I look at the block in my hand, then down at my feet. Two neat piles, of toys, of shoes, clothing. Have I been gathering in my sleep again?

Six men. No women. We get paid better the faster we move, the more we separate. What they do with the stones and rocks, I can't remember: they may have told me once. All I know is I smell like dirt and sweat, like the earth I move all day long, a dusty machine. Their machine.

I eat when they tell me.

Leave when they tell me.

Drink the water they give me to keep from passing out.

The men around me have names like Porter, Mathias, Randolf, Cedric. They change weekly but they all look the same. The flood of names haunts me. Yoder. Robert. D.W. Baxter. I don't know these men. I don't want to.

I'm Kipling. A few years ago I slugged a guy for calling me Kip. I think his name was Thomas. Or Steven.

I have a family.

A wife and two sons.

If I stop, we lose everything.

Without rocks and stones, we have nothing.

Time has become an old friend I no longer call. I've learned to ignore her. The heat bounces off the hard, desert floor, making waves as it moves. Sometimes I imagine a breeze licking my sweat-drenched skin as I stand on the top of a mountain, watching the world go about its quiet business. Imagine watching my kids play. Eating the warm, flaky bread my wife has baked. I imagine a moment when I'm not too tired to do anything but sleep. A moment when my sons see a smile crack from my scorched lips.

147 rocks.

6 stones.

I can barely tell the difference anymore. Every day is the same, each one melting into the next. The fools around me smoke cigarettes they roll themselves as they work in the field.

I despise the smell.

I complain.

More often than I like to think, I catch myself throwing punches in my head.

Out of the corner of my eye I watch one of the others. Mathias. Rock. He reaches up to scratch the growth on his cheek, talking while the rest of us separate.

He's been on the job maybe a week, could be a month. I hate him. Stone. There's a smear of dirt where he rubbed the stubble on his cheek, a dark stubble like my own. It's hard to tell any of us apart. Rock. I don't make eye contact anymore.

It's not even noon and already Mathias has smoked fifteen hand-rolled cigarettes.

He laughs at something he said, triggering coughing.

Five minutes of coughing.

I put stone twenty eight on the appropriate pile.

He reaches into his shirt pocket and pulls out another cigarette. Sixteen. It sits on his lip, bouncing up and down as he chatters away. I try not to listen but his words reach my ears regardless.

"Kip. Hey Kip, man. Do you have a light? Matches? Anything?"

I reach down for a rock.

"Kip, man. Are you stupid or something? Shit. I need a light."

He's closer now, his cigarette still jogging between his lips. Running his thumb and forefinger against his other palm, he strikes an imaginary match and presses it up to the end of his cigarette.

"What?" I mumble as I grasp the rock.

"I've run out of matches. I need a light. You got one?"

He's looking at me.

We're alone, or as alone as two people can be in an open field.

I imagine cocking my fist back and taking a swing, my fist landing squarely against his jaw, the hand-rolled cigarette flipping off his lips, tumbling onto his chest as he hits the sun-beaten earth, dust rising in wisps around him.

I look down at my hand, shaking, grasping a rock.

I turn and place it on the pile. Rock.

THE PACE OF OUR FEET

Waiting and watching
the people all walking around.
The city is singing the busiest sounds.
I'm cross-eyed and stubborn,
but mother taught me to listen
to the whistling of the birds.

We've been losing count.
Why's it so hard to slow down,
when you're singing the busiest sounds?
Lift your lips to my cheek
and walk next to me,
as we slow the pace of our feet.

Now winter is fading,
and life keeps on playing its song.
We're trying our best just to follow along,
so I'm quitting the opera.
I'm done with this dramatic race.
Let's move to Montana for a five-minute break.

We've been losing count.
Why's it so hard to slow down,
when you're singing the busiest sounds?
Lift your lips to my cheek
and walk next to me,
as we slow the pace of our feet.

We're under a spell,
a spin,
a turning,
and I am learning to stop
And watch
The waves
Break
Over the rocks.
I'm learning to stop.

Cause we've been losing count.
Why's it so hard to slow down,
when you're singing the busiest sound?
Why's it so hard to slow down?

lyrics by Justin Tam & Jamie Bennett

45

The Pace Of Our Feet
Oil on Canvas
2008
30 x 30 in
Sara La
Nashville, TN
www.sara-la.com
sara@sara-la.com

THE VOW

by Joel Fry

Winter keeps fading
through the windows,
the curtains, your hair.
The susurrus of birdsong can be
heard through the tides of traffic,
through my shadows when I sleep.
My dreams are soundless
explosions. The trains screech
like they will run until dawn,
till varied voices wake us
from the next room.

Night is still eternal, restless
in its machinery. We will never
catch up with what we owe
this world. The piles of bills
have their monopoly on my fear.
All the old endings keep us
empty handed and looking
for more light.

We have been here
before, in early spring,
when all we needed
was each other
and the warmth
that spans the distance
of touch. The sparrows
danced like dervishes
on trampolines.
We talked nonstop, chanting
the busiest sound,
relentless in our pursuit
of the ghosts between us.

The sun went down.
We found belated rest amid the
noises of traffic, and within
our bodies we knew a single
meeting place, a place we had
always known, a final step
before twilight, a union
that keeps its vow, its promise
this moment always sounding.

STANDING ON THE OCEAN

Judy ran circles around the boys.
She was a fireball from Illinois.
When it was quiet,
she was the noise.

She clapped her heart and beat her hands,
somehow she could understand
the pull, the tugging on her soul.

She was old enough,
young enough but old enough to know
good things come and good things go.
She was old enough,
young enough but old enough to say
good things come and good things go away.

She crawled her way through the crowded streets
with a ring in her ear and an eye for the weak.
She was a daughter,
she was a priest.

So, beat your hands and clap your hearts,
and maybe you will understand your part.
It's not too late to start.

Everything in motion,
everyone is still.
Standing on the ocean,
or floating on the hills.

She was old enough,
young enough but old enough to know,
good things come and good things they will go.

lyrics by Justin Tam & Jamie Bennett

Judy
Acylic, Graphite, and Ink on Canvas
2008
38 x 38 in
Myles Bennett
New York, NY
bennettmyles@gmail.com
http://www.flickr.com/photos/mylesbennett/

LONGONE'S FIRE

by Brandon Boyd

In the darkened wood, the curious Moon spies through the trees at two travelers, a Hermit and a Fool, silent by a ring of stones. The fool, Random Voight, stands flummoxed, waiting here between his human life and what's-to-come. The hermit, Jonathan Longone, reluctant bodhisattva, damned to shuttle souls between the planes, kneels by the firepit arranging twigs. He stacks them neatly in squares, building layer upon careful layer of the delicate tinder. Finally he speaks: "Tell me your story, Random Voight."

"What part?" Random Voight doesn't understand why he is here. But here he is, in this dark forest with this strange shrouded man.

"Tell me about isolation and the feminine principle."

"Something imagined or. . ."

"No, tell me about life, as you have known it."

Life. What did Random know about life? He tries to remember. "There was a girl."

"Interesting. An extant human?"

"Seemed like it."

"What did she look like?" One small twig overlapping another, and so on, and so forth.

"Look like. . .I really can't recall."

"You'll have to come up with something. So I can get a picture. Visualize."
Now larger twigs, stacked gently in a rising square.

"She was like. . .some goddess-in-training, the aura of a drum circle, the crackle of rocks in the desert, clouds on eastern mountains…."

"Yes, I get it." Jonathan Longone has little patience for poetry, after all these years, after all the transitions. Now he lays dry branches against his chimney of wood. Almost ready. "Did she have a name?"

"Judy."

"Judy. Goody." Jonathan Longone strikes a match to his effort and sits, straight and still, as Random Voight recalls his tale.

"I couldn't get on with things. I kept looking under rocks, in the street, in drugs and fairy tales. Something was missing. Tough spot to be in at nineteen, just a boy, nothing more. '

"I found her at a performance of some Buddhist monks at a prestigious university I did not attend. Found her. . .more like she found me. But she wasn't looking. Anyway, it was intermission. The chanting of the monks had left me feeling charged and airy. I drifted through the crowd alone, a long-haired Holden Caulfield adrift in the rye.

"Then she appeared. Emerged. Her eyes came first, ancient flaming pools of amber, framed by red, restless ringlets of hair. Her skin was warm, undulating, pale with a hint of olive. She was light of frame, but room-encompassing.

"Anything resembling fear or me evaporated, and I engaged her."

They met eyes and stood, staring into one another amidst the roiling crowd. Far from speechless, though, he spoke, "You're beautiful."

"So are you."

"I've never seen a woman like you." She laughed and flashed joy. She stayed with his left eye, and he fell into her gaze.

"What am I like?"

"You're like some ancient princess. You're changing me."

"Too bad. I'll never know what you were like to begin with." Silence and the gaze. She laughed again. ""Do you have a name?"

"Random. Random Voight."

"Random Void?"

"Voight."

"That's really your name."

"My mother was a physics teacher – your eyes. . .I can't stop. . . ."

"You don't have to stop. And my name's Judy."

"Judy. Amazing."

She squinted and scanned his face, "Are you high, Random?"

"No. Well, yes, but that doesn't. . .I'm normally high, but I don't normally do this."

"Talk to people?"

"Stare down strange women."

Still the gaze. "Am I so strange?" How did he know what she meant? "What do you 'normally' do?"

"I read. Think about things. And walk."

"You walk?"

"I don't have a car – May I ask you. . .what are your ethnic roots?"

"My roots?"

"Your people. Your ancestors. Your ethnic roots."

"I'm Irish and Persian."

Again she got him, like the blast of a furnace door thrown open in winter. "Who are you?"

"I'm Judy." She shuffled coyly, like he already knew and she knew it.

"But you're *more*. . . ."

Her laugh flared from the corners of her mouth as she sang, "Ground control to Major Random."

"Don't mock, I'm trying to *know*." He furrowed his brows and tried another tactic. "Where are you from?"

"You mean back here on Earth?"

"Yes, damnit."

"I grew up in Chicago, but I live here now."

"Chicago! I grew up in Waukegan, on Lake Michigan."

"Well, butter my toast." The lights flashed in the auditorium lobby. "How are the Khenpos treating you?"

"What?"

"The monks? The chanting guys in the orange robes?"

"Oh. Great. I'm grateful to them."

"For what?"

"For leading to this."

The lights flashed again. "Back to Eternity now, Young Mr. Void."

"Can I. . .can we. . .?"

She reached with a finger and touched him behind his left ear. A pop of static shot down the base of his spine. "We'll meet again, don't know how, don't know when. . . ." She winked as she backed into the absorbing crowd.

"She sounds nice." Now a small fire dances in that darkened space under the trees. Jonathan Longone sits in a half-lotus, one hand squared on his knee, the other holding his chin, barely visible through the shadows and the cowl. He seems to be smiling.

"Nice?"

"Yes. Nice. I like the 'red restless ringlets' of hair. The amber eyes and the skin, too. Very nice." Tongues of flame lapping eager boughs. "So you didn't see her for some time after that."

"No. I thought I never would again. I can't remember what she really looked like. It's screwing with me."

"You're doing great."

"Gee, thanks. What exactly am I doing great at?"

The patient woodsman places a larger log now into the blaze-to-be. "Don't get irritated, Mr. Voight. I'm just doing my job."

"Which is? How did I get here?" Random sees shapes on the shimmering air as the fire grows.

"We'll get to that. Right now I want to hear more about this goddess. You didn't see her for some time after that."

"No. Only in my head."

"Judy whirled through my thoughts as the days moved away from her. I wrote odes to her essence, placed her on a mythic pedestal where she enveloped the stars and carried me with her. I played the blissful Fool, impelled by her image through unknown days.

"Out of the blue, I started meeting women. Like never before, they seemed drawn to me. I was filled with alien confidence. I felt powerful and free. I fell in with a strange Wiccan actress who loved LSD, unneutered cats, and cunnilingus. I met a soft-spoken Christian girl from Texas who played the upright bass; we made out in her car in the rain and she explained the lineage of Jeshua according to the Bible. There was a deaf girl who loved to dance, a thick punk poetess with a bar in her tongue, an alcoholic Cherokee seamstress. Wonderful ladies every one of them, oceans to be explored. I rode the rapids of a mad bohemian fantasy on a raft of false knowledge.

"All the while, I thought of Judy.

"But even the powerful must eat. So I took a job, as people often do. I worked in the café at a bookstore, serving soup.

"One day, while clearing tables, I encountered her again, a red, restless flame, eating a scone and reading Krishnamurti."

"Judy!"
She looked up and smiled. "It's you."
"I'm so glad. . .I can't. . .you're here again."
"In this café?"
"In front of me."
"You work here?"

"I pretend to. How's that Krishnamurti treating you?"

"Great. I like his shitty, cosmic attitude. It boggles the mind."

"You like to have your mind boggled?"

"I love a good boggling."

He pulled up a chair. "Judy. . ."

"Random."

"I haven't stopped thinking about you. It's been months."

That familiar crackle now. "A month or two, yes."

"I want to see you more."

"You haven't seen me?"

"Can I have your phone number? Can I call you? Can I spend some time with you? Can we do something?"

"What are we doing now?"

"Judy..."

"Random," she held up the book, "what is there to do?"

"How about we just indulge in some Being."

"Isn't that what we're doing now?"

"Please."

She paused and he fell down deep in those eyes. "That would be Cosmic."

So they met again in a tree in the park and smoked some grass while people passed below.

"You're my favorite person, Judy."

"How long have you known me?"

"That doesn't apply here."

"As you say, sir."

"I mean it. I want to be here when I'm ninety."

"In this tree?"

"In this tree, smoking this joint."

"I like you too, Random."

"This goes way beyond that."

"You are a silly man."

"Maybe. Wouldn't you like this in a thousand years? Or maybe just later in life? I mean, am I getting to you the same way here, or what?"

"What does that mean?"

"Do you want me?"

"Can I have you?"

"Yes."

"Random. . ." He leaned into her and found her lips. At first she hesitated. Then she met him, and a kaleidoscopic flow burst loose between them.

"Now we're talking." Jonathan throws a pine bough onto the blaze.

"Don't be a lech. That kiss changed my life. She really got into me."

"Everything changes your life. In the end – here we are."

"Which is where?"

Again Jonathan Longone evades the crucial question. He holds long fingers over the heat of the fire. "What happened then, to this Mystic Princess of yours?"

Random Voight winces. "I don't know. She moved on."

"She moved on."

"I couldn't hold her."

"You couldn't get her naked."

"No. She wouldn't."

"Why not?"

"She must have sensed my lack of focus." Random stares at the runes in the fire.

"Judy and I continued to spend time together. I met her family. We went to drum circles and sweat lodges. We pretended we were Brahma's dream, which we were and were not and all that.

"All the while, though, our meetings had a sporadic non-committal quality. You see, despite the obvious heat between us, Judy would never acquiesce to a sexual relationship. I must confess, I never broke ties with the other girls in my life. I, fool that I was, failed to see the connection.

"One night I went to see a production of *Mother Courage* at a small playhouse above a pizza shop. I went alone, just like I used to do things. I wandered invisibly through the crowd. And somewhere along the way, I ran into Judy."

"What are you doing here?"

"Watching a play."

"You should have told me. We could have come together."

"We didn't have to."

"Great. Here we are."

"Random. . . ." Before she could say it, a tall, tattooed young pharaoh stepped into view and put his arm around her waist. Random felt his entire existence blotted out in his shadow.

"Hey." The pharaoh's gaze stayed with Judy, all sex and origin. And power.

"Calvin, this is Random."

"Yeah, how you doing, man?" The Pharaoh never took his eyes off Her.

She smiled sheepishly and said, "I'll see you later, Random."

He couldn't quite process this. "Can I talk to you, Judy?"

"Random, why don't you go see one of your girlfriends?"

"I want to see you."

"Some other time."

"But. . ."

The pharaoh spoke, still focused on Judy: "Go on now, man. Judy's busy."

"I'll see you later, Random." They took each other's hands and disappeared into the theatre.

Random didn't make the second act.

"Ouch." Jonathan Longone ponders the burn he received from the burning stick in his hand.

"Yes. That did me in."

"And after that?"

"I avoided all contact. Are you going to tell me what I'm doing here?"

"You're telling me." Jonathan feeds the offending branch to the bonfire.

"I don't know what that means."

Flames dance five feet high now. Jonathan Longone spreads his arms wide.

"Burn, baby, burn."

"I couldn't face her. I couldn't deal with the facts. The freedom, the power I loved – was she taking that away from me? Could she? What had I done? I felt helpless and empty without her attention. What did that make me? I couldn't rest. So I left.

"I moved to Chicago. I took a few rides around the sun. I surrendered to necessity and took a full time job as a sales associate at a big box retail chain. I rented a room in an apartment leased by an eccentric Asian woman named Ellen. Ellen liked Sade, Sting, mentholated cigarettes, England, and too much pancake makeup. She once had a mildly successful band in Prague. The arrangement worked fairly well as I was rarely home and otherwise kept to myself.

"I reverted to my old isolation. Invisible. Silent. I didn't attempt contact with women. I resolved to live as a man of knowledge and nothing more.

"One Friday, Ellen told me she had a friend coming in for the weekend. It made no difference to me. Like I said, I mostly worked and kept to myself.

"I did my time that Friday. At the end of the day, the bus dropped me in front of my building as always. As I walked to the stoop I noticed obsidian ringlets of hair. A woman in a navy pea coat sat there, playing my guitar and reading from a copy of *Prometheus Rising*. Then I saw her eyes. Judy. It was Judy."

"You're Ellen's friend?"
"Hi there, Random."
"I can't believe this."
"Good to see you too."
"I'm in shock here."
"I'll give you a minute."
"How. . . have you been?"
"Great."

"Where have you been?"

"Let's see. Since last I saw you, I went to college in Athens. . ."

"Greece?"

"Georgia. Then I escaped to New York, then Europe. I met Ellen in Prague. I backpacked through India. Oh, and I saw Levon Helm put on a killer show at the Ryman Auditorium."

"Far out."

"Not really. Same old place."

"I'm speechless. Let's go inside so I can regroup."

They met Ellen out that night for food and revelry. Eventually, Ellen decided to call it quits and left the two old sojourners to catch up on lost time. They got kicked out of the late night bars and ended up talking under an awning in the rain.

"You seem sadder now, Judy."

"Not sad. Just experienced."

"What happened to 'the Egyptian god' you were with the last time I saw you?"

"He was just a guy."

"One of many I presume."

"How can you judge?"

"I can't. Now. I tried to then."

"Why?"

"Why? No idea."

"Everything you ever saw in me, all that epic stuff about eternity and royalty, and still you end up hung up on possessive romance."

"Yeah. I hadn't grown into my ideals, I suppose."

"Have you now?"

"Probably not. Hell, I think I have fully forsaken those ideals. It just turned out to be so much shite."

"Wow. It's like you've given up."

"I have given up."

"Why?" She laughed a laugh of compassion and grief. "Why, Random? Because you discovered I was way ahead of you? I mean, if you're going to quit, do it right. You're still running the race. You're just letting your heart die."

"I told you how I felt then. . ."

"About me?"

"Yes."

"No. About something I awoke in YOU. Maybe I started the fire, but you have to tend to that. You are the keeper of the fire."

"You would never let me touch you."

"I let you."

"Erotically. I wanted to be naked with you. I wanted to feel you all the way through."

"Me and all those other girls."

"They weren't you."

"You never stopped seeing them."

"Was that it? You wanted monogamous commitment?"

"No, Random."

"You had other guys. Why not me?"

"I didn't want to destroy you."

He couldn't respond to that.

"Random, I thought as much of you as you did of me. I think the same of you now."

They flew into each other then, lips, tongues, arms. They absorbed each other there under that awning in the rain.

They took a cab back to the apartment. As they neared the building, they noticed flashing lights, a bit of commotion. Police cars, two of them, outside the building. They got out of the cab and climbed the stairs to the apartment. Ellen was standing at the door talking to two uniformed officers.

"There's really not much we do about burglaries like this, ma'am. Just sign here and we'll file the report."

"Thank you, officer."

"Ellen, what happened?" They all had tear stains on their faces now.

"Some crack-addled fucks broke into the apartment."

"What did they get?"

"They got my stereo and my camera equipment. They took your guitar, too."

"My guitar! Shit, I loved that guitar."

Judy held his arm. "Let's go have a look around."

The place was trashed. They had done a nice job of it. They had taken the cash out of Random's bureau as well.

"I can't believe this," Ellen fumed through plumes of menthol. "I just can't believe this!"

Judy put her arm around her friend's shoulders. "Just get some rest, my dear. We'll deal with it in the morning."

"You mean in the afternoon. You two made a night of it." Ellen kissed Judy on the forehead and retired to her bedroom.

Judy and Random sat in the living room. "Some night," he said.

"Some night."

"My parents gave me that guitar. I learned to play by ear on that guitar. It sang to me."

"They did you a favor, Random."

"How's that?"

"Good things come and good things go." She took him by the hand into his bedroom. They lit a candle and took off their clothes and sat facing each other. As the gazed deepened, the universe imploded. Visions appeared. He saw in her an old, old man. She saw in him an innocent little girl. Random Voight felt life and fullfillment They touched hands, then she climbed into his lap. They stayed like that until they passed into exhaustion, still wrapped in each other's senses.

When he awoke, she was gone. He never saw her again.

"I think I get it now. She probably never existed. Maybe I didn't either. We were just the interplay of light and shadow, the sustaining force of form. The crackle of heat on rocks in the desert."

"You existed." Longone emits patience, calm, understanding.

"No, I think…Judy was an image that grew inside of me, from the base of spine out the top of my head. I can summon her if I sit very still."

The wind blusters and the fire sways.

"She was me and now I am free."

Jonathan Longone places the final log on the fire. "It was good to be alive. It was good to be in a body."

"I'm ready."

"Yes." The fire flickers low now in that effervescent copse. The calm air mingles with the cool sounds of night. Jonathan Longone sits in half-lotus, spine straight, eyes affixed on that eternal flame. Somewhere in his shroud he smiles. "Good story, Random Void."

Random doesn't reply. He is no longer there. His story came and went. Random Voight is nowhere …

In the darkened wood, the Moon peers through the trees at the thoughtful Hermit, animated by shadows of Longone's fire.

ITALIAN WINE

He signed up in the month of May,
grabbed his boots from the infantry.
and I got a letter from Germany.
It said, "Dad I'm fine,
the nurse is nice, but
sometimes it's hard breathe at night.
I'm sorry for leaving without
saying goodbye, that night."

Raise your glass to all the war-bound sons and
hold on tightly to the ones you love.
Italian wine may remind you of the past, but
a billion bottles can't begin to bring it back,
so hold on tightly to your glass,
hold on tightly to your glass now.

Sometimes, I hide under the desk,
shake my head as I reminisce.
Time's like a train
I've been trying to catch,
but the seasons fill these empty rooms with
dust as deep as Egypt's tombs.
I'm tired of winter,
I'm ready for June.

Raise your glass to all the war-bound sons and
hold on tightly to the ones you love.
Italian wine may remind you of the past, but
a billion bottles can't begin to bring it back,
so hold on tightly to your glass,
hold on tightly to your glass.

I hope that it won't be your last,
so hold on tightly to your glass.
I hope that it won't be your last,
'cause we're not ever coming back.

We're all slipping through the cracks.

lyrics by Justin Tam & Jamie Bennett

Bound
Wine, Ink, and Colored Pencil on Paper
2007
22 x 30 in.
LA Bachman
Nashville, TN
www.labachman.com
la@labachman.com

Italian Wine

by Q Bennett

Morning Mulling

Conner's room has been left alone. I walk inside for the first time in months, feeling as if it were the room of an old best friend. Dirty clothes, a closet full of near emptiness, and the smell of incense and cigar smoke kneaded into the carpet. A bookshelf holds some schoolbooks and old poets.

Cross-legged on the floor, I sit as if he were in front of me, a little boy, mind running with his tiny legs. He played many a game of poker here late at night with his imaginary friend Jethro Wilcox the Fifth.

"Jethro," he would say, "is a refugee of the French Revolution."

How Conner knew about the French Revolution, I haven't the slightest idea. I can't imagine his learning about it in school, nor can I picture my ten-year old son and his friends playing hopscotch or tether-ball on the playground while having a pleasant conversation about European social upheaval.

Regardless, his mom and I were constantly chuckling. When he was eight years old and learned what his father drank everyday, Conner told his teacher that he had found a cure for the common cold—alcohol. I can imagine the look on the teacher's face—eyes popped, cheeks red as meat, lips pursed and about to explode.

Somehow, his body and mind always knew when to kick into hyperactive contentiousness. Late at night, before bedtime, mom and I practically comatose, he would run around the house, making weird noises and outrageous claims, such as "Hey everyone! Hey everyone!" his mother and father his only audience, "I have the best idea!"—with a look on his face as if the world of meaning depends upon his great idea's fulfillment— "We should go on an adventure to the zoo and steal a snake! Then we can eat him for dinner! Mom, what do snakes taste like?"

Though there are many memories, I can't remember the two of us ever doing much together or even talking, unless he needed to be punished. He was always closer to his mother than me. And unlike most children who try to communicate with a removed father, he never tried to impress me. Occasionally, he and Karen would garden together. Of course, weed pulling led to dirt throwing, and I could hear their laughs through my window as I lay upstairs half drunk and listening to Groucho Marx on the radio.

"Hey, I'm going for a walk with the dog," Karen says as she swings open the bedroom door and paces by, leaving me sitting and waking me from my thoughts.

"Ok, but don't let Milis near that damned pitbull." She carries on down the hallway and out the front door, whistling. Oh, how she can whistle—curls my ears inward and bounces them to her beat.

I walk outside carrying a glass of wine and sit on the front porch in the chair my son made for me on my fortieth birthday. It creaks like it's older than it is and is already about to fall apart, not the best engineering, but Conner was merely thirteen when he made it. Like a child, I linger in my observations—the sopping hot air, the pigeons haloed in the sun and poking around on the telephone poles across the street. Our cats have been engaged in a staring match with them all morning. I imagine the pigeons all singing Dizzy Gillespie in a round, "If I'm feeling tomorrow like I'm feeling today, I'm gonna' pack my bags and make a getaway" for the hundredth time.

"I wish you would, you rat bastards!" I reply. And then I realize I am that old man on the front porch yelling obscure slurs at God knows who.

The sun speckles the grass with light, and the leaves move with the wind like drunkards. And I can't get that old Whitman out of my head: "Underfoot the divine soil. Overhead the sun." Conner used to read his stuff. He would waltz about the house, quoting *Leaves of Grass*. For this reason, I suspected he might be a bit of a nance. Then he brought home some long skirted girl with pigtails and specs to work on a poetry project. He winked at me as they walked into his room. Proud as I was, I thought the gesture might be a little too cocky for a sixteen-year old. So, like any loving parent, I told her to go home, yelled at him for a while and grounded his ass for a month. Unfortunately, punishing simply allowed him to do what he loved to do—read in his room for hours.

I hear Karen's whistling again. Then I see her head pop around the corner of the driveway bushes, as she sneaks back with a letter in hand.

"I can *hear* you over there, whistling like an elementary school janitor."

"Another letter from Germany, Cole! It is addressed to you and 'for your eyes only,'" making the best imitation she can of a military commander, with that cute look and tone she gets when she makes her voice deep—chin propped out, head bobbed down, brows furrowed.

"Heheh." I give her a sly "you should be jealous" look and set down my glass of wine. Inhaling the wet air, I unfold the envelope and expose its content. Eexhaaaale.

Dear Father,

I awoke my first morning in Foggia, Italy to the cold wind slapping my face, bringing dust thick as the marshes that surround it. We arrived in Foggia from Naples in November, carried by USS General Richardson over the Atlantic. We had only three submarine warnings, two torpedo sirens, and one man overboard. Somehow, he decided that urinating off the side of the ship during a storm was a good idea.

Foggia is constantly smiling but constantly kicking you in the ass. According to the guy a bed over, David Gertrude, a Jewish German (the poor bastard) who has become popular here for his mother's matzo balls, the actual meaning of Foggia is derived from the Latin word "favea," which translates as" "pit." A pit indeed, and to make matters worse, the devastation we wreaked upon it to make it our primary base has left a formidable impression. Thus, I have come to the conclusion that the beauty of Foggia lies not in its landscape but in its inhabitants.

Each weekend we stayed with families that took us in as their own. And every time, I found it difficult to believe that I was actually dining with an Italian family, people who were once thought to be our enemy. The look in their eyes said we are the same. Though, their children half my age were drinking me under the table. As you probably know, they actually allow kids to drink here. Of course, it is only to be consumed with a meal and only wine, but still, at first I thought it was insane. Gradually, however,

I realized that these kids probably have a better respect for alcohol than any of us drunken air corpsman out here.

Yet now, instead of an Italian dining room full of bellowing voices and reaching hands, I sit in a hospital bed surrounded by bleeding oily bodies and sobering screams. And Yugoslavia is even colder than Foggia, where we burned 100 octane fuel for heat, which I cursed for its stench. Now, I would give anything to have it warming up my toes and smelling up this blood rancid room.

I am a member of a heavy bombardment group, flying B-17s (the Flying Fortress). Our last military operation, and supposedly the most prominent we've attempted, has left me with two shattered knees, two fingers short, and a broken hip. I can, however, finally rest. And I can write. Difficult, though, because the missing fingers on my right hand directly affect my ability to etch comprehensible scribbles onto my page.

It hasn't all been so grim, though. A few weeks ago or so, I am not sure when exactly, as details such as time have become rather dim, we had a short vacation in Bari, Italy, just southeast of Foggia—a fleeting moment to forget. My comrade Fred and I walked down to the beach, picking up the sand in our fingers and watching it drizzle like sawdust into a pile between our feet. We watched the salty fisherman bring in their catch of clams at the end of the each day. And like beggars at a bar, we gazed as the Italian girls, in all their lustrous mystery, managed to slip into their bathing suits without revealing a snip of flesh.

Always something to say, Fred is the kind whose humor drowns a room full of boisterous soldiers. I'll never forget him. As one of our navigation and radar technicians, he usually has his head buried amidst white wires, which are meant to fool any German trying to foil the radar. He never has a moment off with all those planes coming in and out, sounding like a band constantly marching. Fred can drone for hours along with them in a voice reminiscent of Mulberry, Arkansas' sweet grass and the orange blossoms blowing through Santa Ana, California.

The rest of the time, Fred gabs about women and more women. Always ready to blow a kiss off the tips of his fingers. "These folks in Foggia," as he brought up on more than one occasion, "are practically giving away their daughters. Just last week, I went out with a gal who brought me down to the best Italian restaurant I've been to yet. Next thing I know I'm meetin' her whole damn family, from her great grandmother to her little cousins. Nothin' like that French gal in Switzerland—independent as a street rat." I have no idea if I shall see Fred again. I last saw him about a week ago before we flew out of our base in Foggia. As for me, no sultry story or dire loves yet, save for a cute nurse who smiles every time she passes my bedside. I have yet to catch her name.

I wish I could tell you how the war is going, but none of us really knows. All they tell us are the banal and trite phrases meant to encourage rather than inform, such as "Each day brings us closer and closer to success, gentlemen," or "We're winning this thing, boys—only a matter of time before we send you home." After all the whoops and yippees, silence all but comforts a self-conscious and broken spirit. I try to avoid too much reflection, hoping these wounds will keep my wilted body incapacitated long enough to come home. I am no coward, father, but the flag simply no longer looks the same. Its fabric no longer flows. The pennant no longer sings "to the soul of one poor little child," as Walt Whitman put it in "Song of Banner at Daybreak." I remember reading him with you as a child. Part of me feels like I shouldn't be telling you this—I know we didn't speak much when I was young, but I think you'd understand.

Often, I think of that day—I believe I was twelve years old—we were driving home from church in that gigantic sleek ship of a car, the Chrysler. You and ma were talking, I'm not sure what about, but the only thing I ever heard you say about the your *war came slipping out of your mouth as if it were a habit of saying, only not around me. You said, "Boy, if I'd a known the kinds of things I'd see in the Great War, I would have never joined in the first place." I thought you were a coward for saying it and never understood why you spent so many days up in your room with the door locked, quiet as a mouse. I now know what it is to hold war in one's head.*

Give ma my love, and break the news to her with the correct amount of gravity, respect, and candor.

With love,
Your son Conner Wilcox Holmes
August 15, 1944

I set the letter down. He already seems to picture himself ending up like me—an old prune battling a drawer full of dreadful memories and death. I have prayed my son survives, but now I fret more for his state of mind post-combat.

A fellow once said, "A man must lose his life to gain it."

I must have died a hundred times in those dirt shells on the front lines in the Great War. I arrived in June of 1918 along with what would become a total of 2.1 million American troops, all huddled together with those flipping French, bumberous British, tree-cutting Canadians, and undisciplined ANZAC Australian troops. We spent eternal hours underground, sweat soaked with fear, paled gray with exhaustion. I am still learning how to remember I am still alive.

I remember things in sections—at night in my dreams, clear as sight. First, always in the same scene, always gnawing on my lips in the bunkers. For instance, last night, I was crouched with Bill in the battle over the Somme, talking about all the fictitious women we might marry when we would get home. He would clench his hair with his fists and slowly push it back whenever he spoke.

The memory goes deeper, almost stop motion picture frames. Sand bags used to support the bunkers are all rotted, soiled with mud and urine, baked in the sun for years. Artillery shells slam into the earth ten feet above and fifty yards away. Soot and dirt fall into our hair like rain drops. Tin coffee mugs filled with water and cigarette trays rattle against the table. 'Don't think about the friends that just got blown to scraps.'

Burnt flesh smell lingers and stings my senses. My skin freezes, jaw clenches, and my muscles tense around my bones. I finally awaken as the drone of the fan blows away my thoughts, sensing Karen turn over at six-o-three a.m. or whatever time it may be. Sunlight passes through the blinds, and Karen's fingers pass through my sweaty hair. She knows. She always knows what my mind has been up to. Two years ago, I would have jumped out of bed, out to the porch to scorch another cigarette and gulp my wine. Now, I lie still as a cold snake, letting her hands remind me I am awake, safe.

Karen walks out the door as I finish the letter, sits on my lap, and stares me in the eyes, worried with sweat.

"Conner is fine, hunny. Seriously"

"I wish it didn't require a *seriously*."

I blush. Somehow, all moms sense their child's anguish. It is as if they hear some pulsing siren, blaring thousands of miles away, and in one moment, mothers across the world pray for their sons. And I, half oblivious, lift my glass in a failed attempt to toast a son I once took for granted.

Or maybe it's just that her son wrote a letter from the war, solely addressed to the patriarch, the one who supposedly has more mental strength. What a ludicrous assumption. I spend more nights in fear than a child suspicious of the creepy shuffling in her closet.

"Something happened to him, I know it, Cole."

"He's OK—safe, but in the hospital. He lost two fingers, broke his hip, and smashed up his knees pretty good. But he finally got to fly the bomber!"

"Oh, that's great." She jumps from my lap, grabs the broom that was leaning against the porch's post, and walks around the side of the house.

"Wait up, will ya? Don't you have anything else to say or ask?"

She turns with a gentle smile, "Nope," and keeps walking.

I lift my glass only to stop half way. "Wait a second. What the hell *is* she doing?" I waddle around the house following her hardened feet to find her climbing on an old, crooked chair ready to fall apart any moment. Neck craned, she swats her broom at a bird's nest under the crook of the roof.

"What the hell do you think you are doing, Karen Rochelle?!"

She pays me no attention, only grunts frustration toward the nest. I poke her left knee with my forefinger.

"Look, Karen, if you think I'm gonna' take you to the hospital today...are you listening?"

"Ha!" With a thud, a dirt-clotted nest falls to the ground. She finally looks at me, eyes wide with excitement, a delicious smile spread across her face.

"Come on, kid. Help me down."

Two Kisses And Give me a Drink

Karen and I met at a munitions auction in Ocean City, Maryland when I got home from the war at twenty two years old. She had short hair, wore a knee length skirt, and was looking for the type of single shot handguns her grandfather used in the civil war. What more did I need?

On our second date, we sat below a willow tree in her dad's back yard. The trunk forced my back erect. She sat across from me, watching the night. My hands, like bark, imprinted, cracking, and dry, wished her skinny fingers would touch them. When I was with her, I thought of nothing. No sergeants with angry, demanding eyes. Only her eyes, green like the leaves and yellow like the moon as she caressed my sweaty legs with her toes.

"Damn you look beautiful," I barked.

Silence.

"Sorry, I'm not much for words."

I sat even more still, afraid of making the move I had wanted to make all night. She looked away from me, aloof. Her toes even stopped caressing my legs. I thought she might be losing interest, so I shifted around a bit and fiddled with my hands to protest the tension. Then slowly a smile raised her cheeks, and I thought, "Is she enjoying toying with me?" Suddenly, she leaned up and pressed her body into mine. Then I stopped caring either way.

Years later, my past flooded my thoughts, as if to say

"Hello, remember me (or the you twenty or so years ago)? We still have a card game of War to finish, my friend."

So I drank. Always wine. When the war ended in November of 1918, I was able to travel to Southern France, where the port of Nice lies heavily inhabited and bustling with traveling merchants, though because of the war, not much seemed to be happening. There I was introduced to the European fascination of wine and haven't been able to quit drinking it since.

To begin, I drank on occasion and with friends only. But later in life I found that drinking allowed for a time to reflect and dwell upon its weightier subjects. I drank because of the war, and I drank because I no longer knew my wife, aside from her daily habits and routines. Three times to the bathroom every morning—once to use the toilet, then to the kitchen to cook her eggs with every seasoning one can imagine, once to brush her teeth, then to walk Milis, and finally to shower and apply make-up, which has only been a recent habit as of the last six years, and I hate it. When I met her, she was that oblivious girl that every other girl hated, beautiful without having to try. Twenty years later she woke up counting her wrinkles.

Whatever the excuse for a little drink, exclusion of expression described Karen's and my relationship. All those years we barely acknowledged each other's presence. For that matter, Conner and I were the same, him cooping himself up in his room reading and me hiding under my desk in my room, counting the number of times I lost a man in combat. Then Conner left.

That morning I charged around the house, spitting worry into each room, clamoring down neighbors' doors. I must have looked like a crazed hen who had lost her golden egg. Karen and I looked into each other's wide eyes, and a bevy of mutual misunderstood frustrations was released like captives. Our son was and is gone.

There would be, however, no discussing our rekindled attraction. Words are superfluous in such a moment, more meaningful without having to define or deconstruct them.

Afternoon Amity

I help Karen down from the chair and grab it with a sense of urgent anger, my free hand swinging by my side. "You worry me sometimes."

"Aren't I the one that is supposed to be doing the worrying?"

"You worry enough, Karen."

She looks away smiling as though she is hiding something, and I look at her to catch her eyes. She holds my gaze with pupils that say more than I will ever understand. All I know as a result of this is that she is alright and will talk about Conner when she deems it necessary. She walks toward the front of the house. Again, I follow her with a stoop up the steps and onto the porch.

I sit in the chair that my son made for me, listening to the constant rhythmic cacophony of locusts and those damn pigeons. Maybe they are telling me Conner will be home soon. I hear my wife banging pots and pans together in the kitchen, the water running in the sink, overflowing into a puddle on the kitchen floor. She always forgets to turn it off, and I am too stubborn to care. I hear her whistle Dizzy and Benny Goodman as she jumps in the shower. Crazy woman, she will be a busy bassoon until she dies.

I imagine I am on the beach in Bari with Conner, entering the cool quiet nest of the sea, crabs scuttling along the sand bottom, clapping to the tide. I catch the lip of a wave, and sail down its face. Hello, Conner. I don't know if I will see you again. I understand you less than you think. You see, I feel like I am getting younger each day, more curious about this life, more in awe of what I do not understand, more confused yet understanding than I was at your age. I sit here, asking not "Oh, God, what am I to do?" or "Oh, God, why is it this way?" but, instead, "Ok, God, *how* do I live this life? With what attitude or demeanor do I clothe my old wooden heart?"

I can't blame you for listening to the flag, fighting to uphold it and now doubting it. I did too. I can't blame you for leaving without my consent; I would have left too. I can't tell a boy what to do. Getting him to obey is like man's attempt to tame nature. I've given you to this world. I expect nothing back, but a smile, a few words, and "I love you."

Though, it would be nice to share a cigarette and a glass of wine and talk about those fine Italian women...

or that nice nurse you keep talking about.

EVALINE

She walked down that road.
Who's that man moving slow?
He's got eyes like a crow's
and hands like a ghost's.
Steady, careful,
he'll take all you own.

And he says,
"Evaline, where you goin'?
Where you been?
Evaline, if only
you still knew me,
my Evaline."

There were cracks in the dishes,
there were smiles in the kitchen.
He grew wine in his fields
with fingers that could kill.
Heavy anger is what my senses feel.

lyrics by Jamie Bennett & Justin Tam

Evaline
Graphite, Frosted Mylar, and Paper
2008
13 x 13 in
John Whitten
Nashville, TN
www.johnpwhitten.com
johnwhitten@mac.com

EVALINE

by Kemper McDowell

It was our dream house. It had finally appeared after more than a year of exhaustive searching. I never would have believed that building the resources to buy a two million-dollar home would seem easier than finding a two million-dollar home to buy. I had sold my business for an insanely distorted profit. My wife, Honey, was feeling the biological clock and growing weary of being a teacher. We agreed it was time to bolt from the city and realize my dream of a micro-vineyard. We knew two million wouldn't buy much in Marin, so we had focused on the western part of Sonoma County. But, after fourteen months, we were still searching. The frustration was like quicksand. We had both reached a state of perpetual gloominess. We hadn't even experienced a close call. Then, when we hadn't heard from her in weeks, the agent, Carol Ann, called late one night.

"I think this is the one!" she bellowed.

She was giddy, explaining how happy she was for us and how good things are worth waiting for and that it was karma and on and on. I remained skeptical. I had long since lost count of the number of homes we had seen. Carol Ann scheduled a showing for that Friday. And it was easily worth checking out: 62 acres, 40 of 'em grapes, big house from the turn of the century (no, the one before that), amazing view of the countryside, all for $2.3 million. It sounded too good to be true. But since we were only hoping for half that much acreage, it was with renewed optimism that we left home that Friday morning.

The Golden Gate was engulfed in fog when we crossed the bridge. We were unable to see the tops of the holy spires of engineering that never fail to mesmerize each of us. The weight of a year's worth of frustration seemed lifted as we got north of the city. Honey smiled and the skeptic in me let his guard down long enough to believe that maybe ol' Carol Ann was right. Maybe this was the one.

I took Honey's hand. I kissed it. I knew myself. I knew Honey.

Less than an hour later we had already passed through Petaluma and were turning west toward Sebastopol when she squeezed my hand and asked, "How do you feel?"

"I don't know," I told her, with what felt like a knowing grin, "If it sounds too good to be true, maybe it is."

The farther I got from San Francisco, the better I felt. The air was cleaner. The land was greener. The pulse was slower. I remembered that I felt this way every time I came up here. By the time we passed through Sebastopol, I was feeling downright optimistic. We turned north on a tiny road. We disappeared into the shadows of redwoods. A mile later we turned and crawled up and around a golden mountainside dotted with oaks. The asphalt turned to gravel as switchbacks took us down the other side, finally descending alongside a gentle stream into a dry, flat valley floor. On the distant hillside: grapes.

The stream eventually widened, welcomed by greener grass and small alder trees. There were cattle, sheep, goats and llamas. A stone house sat on the hill overlooking all of them. The road forked, and we turned up the hill toward the grapes we had seen from a couple of miles back. Halfway up the hill I had to arc around a redwood that had grown out into the road, brushing aside the asphalt. I was hooked.

Just before the road curved into an open hillside below acres of grapes, we passed beneath an old gray wooden arch. In it was carved, "EVALINE."

Earlier in the week, Carol Ann had e-mailed all the info she could gather on the place, and I had done a little Internet snooping of my own. The place had been in the McGee family for over fifty years. Mr. and Mrs. McGee were both recently deceased, with an attorney selling the place on behalf of distant family members back east. The lower 12 acre pasture was leased to the Wayne brothers across the road. The asking price was 2.3 and we could only spend 2.

One thing we were not able to determine in the least was the source of the name "Evaline." I was feeling pretty captivated by it and hoping to find out more. I knew that these places often had such names. We had looked at a couple of others. But the name "Evaline" had a grip on me. I couldn't get it out of my mind.

The road gently sloped into a horseshoe of laurels, in the shadows of which sat a century-old Cape Cod-style home straight out of a Steinbeck novel. Spread out below us was the valley we had just crossed. In front of the house sat Carol Ann's Chrysler Behemoth or Ford Colossal or whatever that manstrosity is. She hopped out of it, waving, as we eased down the hill. Honey squeezed my hand. It felt like a defining moment in my life. I felt something that was different. I think it might have been hope.

As I parked behind the Toyota Gargantua, Honey let go of my hand and whispered, "Here we go." We each got out of the car and I immediately felt the unmistakable mucky dank ambiguous smell and disturbing anti-tingle of bad juju, as if a tomb had just been opened. I turned to look at Honey, wondering if she sensed something as well. She was looking at the ground, shoulders slumped, as if she might cry. We were snapped out of our mutual funk by the giggle and boom of Carol Ann's voice.

The tour that followed over the next hour was even more impressive than the photos had been, which was unprecedented in our search. Evidence of recent renovation was everywhere. The place was clearly in poor shape when the McGees passed away, but no longer. I had been watching Honey, so by the time Carol Ann told us the bad news, I knew it was too late. She revealed that the attorney was sticking firmly to the asking price and would not counter a lower offer. It had to be the full 2.3. And now that I had seen the place, I knew it was probably worth closer to three million. I saw the look on Honey's face, and I knew that somehow, one way or another, I was going to have to pull three hundred thousand dollars out of my ass. But I must've had the same look on my face because I was already scheming ways to make it happen.

As we pulled away from Carol Ann standing beside her Chevy Leviathan, I assumed that the earlier wave of bad juju had merely been a premonition of the impending three hundred thousand-dollar reality. I drove very slowly under the "EVALINE" sign and down the hill. Honey took a deep breath and exhaled the words "What now?"

I didn't build a multi-million dollar company by blindly going through the motions. When I got back to the fork in the road, I turned sharply to the right, with Honey mumbling "Where you goin'?" The driveway was just a little ways up the hill and I turned into it, heading for the stone house. "Gonna do a little investigating," I said.

Two men were working on a truck beside the house, where I pulled up and parked. One was a Mexican and the other a tall man with white hair who looked like he would be more at home in Iowa or Nebraska than in Northern California.

"I'm looking for Mr. Wayne," I told them.

"I'm Charlie Wayne," said the white-haired man, who wiped off his hand and shook mine.

The Mexican continued working on the truck. I introduced myself, told him we might be buying the McGee place, that I knew about the lease arrangement on the lower twelve acres and how I thought it would be a good idea to get acquainted. After the appropriate small talk was executed, I came to my purpose. "What about the name, Evaline? You know where that comes from?"

He stole a quick glance toward the Mexican man and said, "No, I wouldn't know anything about that. We only been here seventeen year. That was before my time."

"Well, it's an interesting name."

He just shrugged. He seemed to want to return to his work, and I sensed that our chit-chat was over, so I thanked him and we left.

Our day was done pretty early, so driving back through Sebastopol, we stopped for a late lunch and a beer. Honey was clearly charmed by the old house. We talked about the view, the laurels, and the name "Evaline." One beer led to another. I was gazing blindly at the pedestrian traffic out the window when I realized that the man who just walked past was the Mexican man from the Wayne ranch. "I'll be right back," I told Honey as I rushed out of the bar.

I caught him at the corner and said, "Excuse me, sir, uh….hi…..I saw you at…..you work for Mr. Wayne?"

"Si," he said quietly, unimpressed with my conclusion.

"Um….how are you? Mi espanol no es bueno……..may I …..cerveza?"

"Como esta."

94

"Uh…what's that? I didn't understand."

"You should say 'Como esta — how are you?'"

The message gradually seeped through my thick skull.

"Oh. I see. Como esta?'"

"Muy bien," he nodded, adding, "And then you should say 'Dude, can I buy you a beer?'"

We had a nice laugh over my monolinguality, and I took him inside and introduced him to Honey. Fortunately, his English was very good, and we got to know each other over a couple of beers. His name was Conrado Flores. He came to the United States in his late twenties from Mexico, where he had taught accounting in a university. But, due to the language barrier when he first arrived, he was unable to continue that career. Instead, he was forced to take landscaping and handyman jobs. Thirty years later he was still a handyman. It turned out he had worked for the McGees as well as the Waynes. He told us that he owned some land in Mexico and had been saving up to go retire there one day and build a house on it. I liked Conrado a lot, and safe in the knowledge that Honey was driving the rest of the way home, I was getting loosened a bit by the beer.

But as soon as I worked my way up to the "Evaline" question, his tone changed entirely. "Some things are better not to be talked about," he mumbled as his body language shifted to one of paranoia and conspiracy. "Very sad," he added.

I slowly looked over at Honey's poker face. I leaned in to Conrado, trying to establish rapport by mirroring his body language and told him quietly, "Here's the thing: we might be buying the McGee property and we want to know everything about it. If you worked for the McGees, then you probably know as much as anybody."

He smiled, but just barely. And his eyes sparkled as if he knew far more than he would ever tell me.

As I took out my wallet under the table, I said, "Conrado, you know how much a property like that is worth? It's millions."

He nodded.

"To spend that kind of money, I need all the information I can get." I put two hundred dollars in his hand and whispered, "It's important. I need your help."

Conrado Flores took my money and a deep breath. Then he sat back in the booth, more relaxed. For a long time, he was quiet. His gaze turned downward, as if all his attention were going into his chest and abdomen. Finally, he picked up his beer and took a big long drink as if it were sobering. He looked at me with a calmness, almost condescending, that I hadn't seen earlier.

"Dude," he said, "they started out they were asking 2.5. No one wanted. People look. No offer. And so they drop it. 2.3 and now you are here. But you should know that…if you going to buy the Evaline, then you should know the truth. There is ghost."

I was stunned. Then I sort of chuckled, but there was no breath behind it, so it was more like a flinch. I maintained equilibrium. A ghost. That should be no problem whatsoever for me as I did not believe in ghosts. But strangely, that part of me, that Capricorn part that clings to rational adult sober-minded thought, experienced a division from that part of me that was suddenly reminded of the bad juju upon arrival that morning. Simultaneous with that realization came the excruciating sensation of Honey pinching my arm. Clearly, she was traveling down the same thought process.

Then my body language changed. I snapped out of my buzz and into business mode. I realized I could speak plainly to Conrado. "How do you know about all that, Conrado?"

"I do the repairs on the house," he told us. "I lay tile, paint, everything. The lawyer he come around to see work. He talk. I listen."

It didn't seem wise to mention, even to Conrado, that I thought the place was worth almost three million. "Do you think it'll sell, now that they dropped the price?"

He smiled gently. "Oh, I don't know. I know there is ghost. Person must be right person to live with ghost."

"You're serious about this?"

"Oh yes. It is very serious."

There was a long pause. We each drained our beers. Honey pinched my arm again. The sober-minded rational Capricorn was losing out to the part of me re-living the unsettling chill from earlier in the day.

Finally, I offered, "This ghost, is it the ghost of Evaline?"

Conrado wiped his hands on his pants legs. He seemed to be getting restless. "It is the ghost of the place named Evaline, yes. But it is wrong to think of ghost as one person. Ghost is vibration, does not know itself. Ghost really is two people. Was two people."

"You mean there's two ghosts?" Honey asked.

"Not two ghosts. A ghost. It is two."

"I'm not sure I understand," I told him.

"I can show you ghost," he said, twinkling a bit. "We can go to the Evaline and I show you ghost. You will see it is two. If you buying the Evaline, you should see ghost first."

I brushed Honey's hand away.

"Um....when could we..?"

"Now," he said, without emphasis.

"Right now?"

"Si. Very soon."

The late afternoon sun was lost behind the hills to the west, but night was still an hour or more away. Perplexed and intrigued, Honey and I poked each other a few times under the table until I responded, "But it's not even dark yet. Don't ghosts appear at midnight or in the dead of night or whatever? Do we have to stay up there all night like some kind of stakeout?"

"No, we will not need to be cooking. Seeing will not take long. The midnight is from your ghost stories in the books, the stories that you tell the children. This ghost it is real. It will appear in the moment when the day becomes the night. The time of change from light to darkness. You call it the...the twilight. It is the...the word is...tran...."

"Transition?" Honey threw in.

"Yes, transition."

Somehow I had the feeling that he knew that word.

"The transition is when you will see the ghost."

Then with a coy smile that belonged on a boy of six rather than sixty, he added, "And if you will buy more beer, dude, I will tell you the story of Evaline."

We picked up a six pack across the street and drove west out of Sebastopol again, this time on the threshold of dusk. Feeling entirely sobered by the prospect of seeing a ghost, I drove. We picked up Conrado where he dropped his truck near the Wayne place. He took us up a steep side road we hadn't even noticed. It eventually deposited us at the top of the vineyard, looking down on the entire 62 acres of Evaline. We left the car and followed a path alongside the vineyard to a steep grassy hillside with a direct view of the trail leading up from the house. We sat in the grass about 200 feet uphill. I opened a beer and we each settled into the clingers and stickers of the dry grass, which didn't seem to bother Conrado as much as Honey and me, who were wishing we had brought a blanket.

From our perch we could see across the valley to the last remnants of pink and orange in the west. The hillsides were golden. The laurels were lush. It seemed like a place where I could spend the rest of my life. I knew if I blew this deal, and we returned to our exhausting search, Evaline would forever be known as the one that got away. Determined, enchanted and uncomfortable, the ol' rational Capricorn seemed to be making a comeback. I was far more concerned about bringing my wife out in the middle of nowhere at night with a stranger than I was about any ghost. Then, without introduction, Conrado began his story.

"There were two Mrs. McGees," he started abruptly.

Then, after another sip of beer, he continued, "When I first came to this country I went to work for Mr. McGee. He was married to the first Mrs. McGee. Her name was Evaline. They seemed like a happy couple. Miss Evaline was tall, with white skin and big brown eyes, the Black Irish you call it. When I came to this country my English was not so good. The McGees did not think of me as someone who spoke English, so they were not careful about what they said when I was close. I did not mean to eavesdrop, but sometimes I would be working close to the house and I would hear what they were saying. Miss Evaline, she was much younger than Mr. McGee, and very beautiful. Sometimes Mr. McGee would be very jealous, asking where she had been. He was very protective and suspicious. Over time, Miss Evaline seemed very upset by this. She was not the same. They did not talk the same way as before. She seemed very sad all the time. He seemed very angry all the time."

He paused and took a deep breath. Honey let go of my hand and, looking away, across the void of the valley below, opened a beer for herself.

"This is a very sad story," Conrado said quietly, "it makes me sad to tell it."

I didn't know what to say. Eventually, to break the silence, I mumbled, "Will the ghost come soon?"

"It is not time yet, but soon," he answered.

The last glow of pink and orange disappeared in the west and a gray chill descended on us.

"In time," he went on, "they did not talk much at all. After many years…" he trailed off. He finished his beer and opened another.

"One day, there was a big fight. I was working close to the house and could hear because Mr. McGee was yelling very loud."

Suddenly Conrado got much quieter and leaned in closer, as if afraid of being overheard.

"He was saying that she had been with another man. He called her many bad names. He was saying that she had disgraced their family. I was afraid for her safety because he was so angry, but I did not want to interfere. It was not my place. I went on with my work. All day they would become quiet for a while, then very loud again for a long time. It made me feel very uncomfortable, like I could feel what they were feeling. I finished my work, and I went home. I did not want to hear them any more."

Again he paused and drank. This time, though, he did not continue the story. He looked up at the few stars that had appeared. Then he drank more beer, sitting silently as if his tale was finished.

I was just about to speak up when Honey beat me to it.

"What happened?" she asked gently.

"The next day they were gone," he sighed, turning away.

"They were gone?" I asked, eyebrows raised.

"She," he said quickly, "she was gone. When I got there the next morning, Mr. McGee was in a terrible state. He did not have to tell me that she was gone or that she was not coming back."

"What happened to her?" Honey asked him.

"No one knows," he said, smiling ever so slightly at her. "She was never seen around here again."

"Do you think he killed her? Is she the ghost?" I suggested, grimly.

"No, nothing like that. Miss Evaline, she just run away. Like I told you before, this ghost, it is two."

"I still don't understand that. It's not the same as two ghosts?"

"Maybe ghost is not what you think."

As the three of us sat quietly drinking, a small gray owl came from the ridge behind us, over our heads, and glided down the slope of the vineyard to the laurels near the house. It never made a sound. Neither did we. The dropping of jaws was confirmation enough.

"I'm cold," Honey said, leaning against me.

I liked the mountain chill. It was sobering. I had a house to buy, and I still didn't believe in ghosts.

"What about the second Mrs. McGee?" I asked, casually.

"For many years, Mr. McGee was very sad. His heart was broken. I think he was sick in his head. He save everything, all the pictures, her clothes. He had me build the wooden arch and had me carve her name in it. He thought it would welcome her home when she came back to him. But she never came. He was a very disturbed man. I did not like the way I felt when I was here. That was the time when I also began to work for Mr. Wayne across the road. After a few years, there was a sudden change. Mr. McGee had a girlfriend. He made me take everything that had belonged to Miss Evaline and put it all in a box. Then I put the box away in the attic like he told me. I asked if he wanted me to take down the wooden arch, but he said no. He said that he was moving on with his life, to marry another woman, but this vineyard would always be called 'Evaline.' In a few months, Mr. McGee got remarried. Her name was Sarah. She was a very nice lady, not as young and beautiful like Evaline, but very nice. Mr. McGee seemed more relaxed having a wife his own age. He was not so jealous and angry all the time. I never heard them have a fight. They seemed happy together. A nice older couple. I did not mind coming to work here anymore. Sarah would talk to me, ask about my wife, and it did not bother Mr. McGee. He always hated for Miss Evaline to talk to me at all. But, with Sarah, he did not mind. She was my friend."

He paused, looking down the hill. "We have only a little bit of time before what you came to see. I will tell you more, but this part is...this is the part that is very hard for me to tell you because it is so sad. A few years ago, the second Mrs. McGee, Sarah, she began to get the...dementia? Yes? You call it...."

"Alzheimer's," Honey offered.

"Yes. How do you say...?"

"Alzheimer's"

"Alzymer, yes. My friend Sarah she had the Alzymer and she lose her memory. It became worse and worse. Some days she could not remember her own name. Mr. McGee did not talk about what was happening to his wife. She would wake up in the morning and look around the house for clues to know who she was. She did not recognize me or even her own husband. One day, when the…when it was very bad, somehow Mrs. McGee she got into the attic and she open the box with all of the belongings of Miss Evaline. She see all the pictures of a beautiful young woman and she thinks that it is herself, many years before. And she reads the name, 'Evaline.'

"I did not know this at the time. I only knew that she told me she had a way to remember, that she had left herself clues to know herself. She seemed to be feeling better. I did not know what really was happening. I did not know until later, when I found the box. This was the time when my wife died. She was sick for a long time and I was gone from work. I was not here for many weeks. After my wife passed away, I returned to work here one morning. I was with Mr. McGee at the edge of the vineyard. Mrs. McGee, Sarah, came out of the house. She walked up the trail toward us and Mr. McGee said, 'Good morning, Evaline.' And she answered him, 'Good morning.' Then he said, 'You remember Conrado, don't you?' She looked me over like she was not sure. She said, 'Good morning. I'm Evaline.' I didn't know what to say. I looked over at Mr. McGee, who was smiling, and I just said to her, 'Good morning.' I was very uncomfortable. After she went back to the house, I said to Mr. McGee, 'Is she okay, sir?' He told me that she was doing much better and the name was nothing to worry about.

"After that, she had good days and bad days. But even on the good days, she was never Sarah. It was always 'Evaline.' I felt like that I should tell someone about this. But I did not know who to tell and I knew that it was not my place to do so. I tried to talk to Mr. McGee, but he told me not to worry. He said that the doctors were helping Mrs. McGee and I should not be concerned. He said that I was worried too much because of my own wife dying recently. But it was not that. I knew that something was wrong. I knew that Mr. McGee was doing nothing to stop Sarah from thinking that she was Evaline. I knew that he was encouraging her, that he was loco and obsessed with Evaline, who left him, but I told no one. He was trying to make Sarah believe.

"Then something very strange happened. They began to fight. Mr. McGee began to be angry. He sounded jealous, like before with the real Evaline. I knew that Sarah was fighting for her identity. I wanted to talk to her but Mr. McGee did not want the two of us to be friends any longer. He told me not to talk to her. He said it was because of her condition, but I knew the real reason. He did not want anyone reminding her that she was Sarah, not Evaline.

"One morning I was working on the irrigation up the hill away from Mr. McGee when Mrs. McGee came out of the house. She was looking very confused and afraid. She approached Mr. McGee very slowly. It was clear to me that she did not know him. He reached out his hand for her, saying, 'Evaline.' She turned back toward the house and moved quickly away when he said, 'Don't you know me?' The look of terror in her face, the confusion, it was the most disturbing thing I have ever seen. You will see for yourself in a minute or two."

"That soon?" I sat up.

"Oh yes. Very soon now."

Honey leaned in closer. She clutched my hand. The gray hillside darkened. Conrado went on.

"Mr. McGee was very angry. He followed her into the house. I could hear him yelling. It was like he was reliving that day when he fought with the real Evaline, and so was I. She was crying. He was yelling. I didn't know what to do. It was not my place to say anything to Mr. McGee."

I knew that if I didn't chime in, Honey would. She was fidgeting. So I gently urged him, "Why was it not your place?"

Through the near-darkness I could detect a slight smile. "Some things are the way that they are."

Honey couldn't hold her tongue. "But you said she was your friend. How could…?"

"Shhh," she was cut off by a suddenly intense Conrado, "this is the time when we should be very quiet."

The wind picked up. I began feeling a little cold. I didn't want any more beer. We sat silently for a couple of minutes. I began to get irritated. I thought about the absurdity of being out there in the cold on the side of that mountain. I thought about Conrado, wondering what his angle was. Very quickly I felt like rage was surging through me. I was on the verge of giving Conrado a piece of my mind and starting back for the car when I realized that Honey was crying. At the same time, I recognized that feeling from the morning, that dank unnerving wave of bad juju.

As I was taking a deep breath to calm down, Conrado pointed toward the house and, very quietly but urgently, hissed "There!"

Honey sobbed louder. I held her, rocking with an almost silent, "Shhhh…" as I tried to focus on the pale blue light along the trail below us. She settled a bit as we both leaned forward. The light grew brighter. At times I was sure I detected the shape of a man. But it was very difficult to discern, as the pale blue light seemed to be a part of the dusk itself and there was little contrast. But, still, it was undeniably glowing. Then a second figure, much brighter, appeared from near the house. The first figure seemed to intensify. We were breathless. Both figures glowed brightly and Honey's sobs returned as the second figure moved up the trail toward the first. There seemed to be a hum in the air, like there is near electrical lines.

That and a smell I cannot describe. And then I was him....

.....and she is walking toward me, my beautiful Sarah, the only best friend I have known, who saved me from myself, who rebuilt me so that I might live again, my dear wife with whom I can grow old in peace. My beautiful Sarah approaches me and I say to her, "Good morning, Evaline." And I try to smile, but cannot feel my lips, cannot force even a token grin. She looks at me as if I have betrayed her and I know that I have. She is lost. She does not know whether she is Evaline, Sarah or someone else. I am the one rock she can cling to and I have thrown her back into the chaos. I have denied her the one small slice of peace that she seeks: simply to know with certainty who she is. She lingers a second, as if she wants to believe that she is Evaline, then flees, eyes full of panic and mistrust. Though I do not feel my mouth move, I hear, in my own tortured voice, the words, "Evaline, where you going?" I pursue her. I feel no body walking beneath me. I slide magnetically toward her, propelled by my rage. I grab her by the arm. I tell her she will never leave me again. I loathe myself more and more as each second passes, more with each word spat at her. I want to bolt, out of my self-hatred and into Evaline, who does not deserve my love. I want to escape inside Evaline. And there is only Sarah, who deserves so much more than my love and what she gets is brainwashing by a Pygmalion so perverted, so lost, that he believes it himself. Of the two of us, I am by far the sickest, and her curse includes the blessing of not knowing the man she married. I am blessed with no such ignorance. I know too much. I know myself and myself is the hell I can never escape. I squeeze her arm tighter. "Don't you know me?" Trembling, she backs away, pulling on her arm. I love you, Sarah. I squeeze tighter. Take it, Evaline. Accept me. This is my hatred. Accept it. Take it, Evaline. Swallow my hatred....

I knew who I was. And I knew that I was watching two pale blue lights merging and slowly dimming. I knew that I was back on the hillside sitting between Honey and Conrado. I knew that Honey was sobbing again and wiping tears from her cheeks. So was I. And I knew who I was.

In an instant, the twilight was gone, and we were in pure dark of night. The pale blue glow down the hill disappeared completely. The bad juju did not.

Honey and I were both breathing heavily and sniffling. Conrado was inexplicably calm. We sat there for about a full minute of silence that was finally interrupted by Honey.

"I wanna go home," she said firmly.

We stood up and walked back to the car in silence. I drove, clinging to the steering wheel to keep from trembling. None of us said a word on the way down the hill to Conrado's truck, but before he got out of the car, I asked him wearily, "So what happened to them? The McGees."

"I guess you could say that they went insane together and then they died together. He outlived her by a couple of months, but he was gone already. At the funeral he kept calling her Evaline and even tried to get that put on a gravestone. But they got it right. Most people just thought he was a crazy old man and never gave all that 'Evaline' stuff a second thought. They didn't know the whole story."

"How did they die?"

"Sarah died of complications from her disease, some kinda stroke or something. Mr. McGee had cancer. For a long time. They couldn't treat it. It slowly killed him."

For the first time during our afternoon and evening together, there was an awkward pause. It didn't seem like there was anything left to say. As Honey moved up to the front seat, I motioned Conrado around to the driver's side. He walked around, and I handed him another two hundred bucks.

"Thank you, Conrado. You were absolutely right. If we were going to buy that house, we needed to see...um...see that. Thank you. Gracias."

"No problem, dude. It was right that you should know."

"Why do you keep calling me 'dude' like that?"

"Goodnight, sir. Drive safely."

And he was gone, disappearing into the shadows before I could say another word.

We drove back in silence. Though the evening was young, Sebastopol had grown quiet, as well. Heading east back to the 101, I reached for the radio, but as I did her hand reached for mine and she sighed, "No, please."

We reached the 101 in silence and the bad juju was still with us.

I drove the fifty miles down the 101. Bad juju remained. I couldn't stand it anymore. I was getting irritated. I broke the silence, but all I could manage was, "Did you...?" before she cut me off.

"I don't want to talk about it."

"I'm just saying did..."

"Yes, I saw it. OK? I saw it. Them. It. Whatever."

"But did you...."

"I don't want...."

"Look, something happened to...."

"I don't want to talk about it."

And what that means is that she does not want to talk about it. So we did not. And silence accompanied us across the bridge and all the way home. We never even glanced up at the holy spires of engineering.

As we were getting ready for bed, she finally spoke: "Did you notice that his accent changed at the end?"

"What?"

"Conrado. When he was getting out of the car, he sounded different. More articulate or something, I don't know, but different. I think his accent changed."

"Probably your imagination. Everything was seeming different right about then. It still does."

"I don't think so. Didn't you notice...?"

"I don't think I really want to talk about it."

Don't know why I said that. Maybe it was petty vengeance for when she said the same thing in the car. Maybe, at 42, I was still childish. Or maybe it was just bad juju.

At any rate, it carried over to the following morning. And through the day. And the day after that. And the day after that. Something was different. Honey and I no longer looked at each other in the same way. We felt like we had brought the bad juju of Evaline back with us. We rarely talked about what happened that night. But it was always with us.

After a few days, the trauma, at least, had faded. I began to think a lot about something that Conrado said that night. He said, "Maybe ghost is not what you think."

But I didn't believe in ghosts at all, so I had no preconceptions. The only part of the experience that my Capricorn mind could wrap itself around was that, at one point, Conrado referred to it as a vibration. Loose though it be, that notion at least resembles forces that I know from Physics class. I gradually began to think of the event I witnessed as more vibration than apparition. I certainly saw something down the hill that night, but what I saw is the least of what was there. More disturbing is what I felt. And especially what I knew. I still would not be so bold as to try to define what a ghost is. The skeptic in me is only prepared to admit that what I experienced that night was as real as anything I have ever experienced, and if it was some kind of hallucination, then so could every day of my life be hallucination.

We never discussed making an offer on the house. There was nothing to discuss. We were never going near there again, not even to that part of Sonoma County. Nonetheless, the Evaline property stayed in my mind, and after a couple of weeks, I called Carol Ann and asked her to monitor the situation and drop me an occasional update. A month later she called to inform me the price on Evaline had dropped to 2.1 million.

I held the phone and told Honey the news, adding, "She wants to know if we're still interested."

We had a big laugh over that. It was the first time we'd laughed since we went to Evaline.

A month later she informed us the price had dropped to two million. We began thinking of it as the place that would never sell and wondered how low it would go. We settled back into our own home search. After we heard it didn't sell at 1.9, we very rarely mentioned Evaline. But it was heavy in the silence between us. The Evaline ghost, or whatever it was, had transformed the world that I perceived around me. Before, I didn't believe in ghosts. Suddenly, I was seeing them everywhere. The grim reality of my increased understanding was an awareness that ghosts are around us all the time. And they are not what we are taught they are. They are much more dangerous.

In time, we found a new routine. I was writing a business plan for a new venture. Honey was out of teaching and dedicated full-time to riding horses and finding our dream home. And then the news came from Carol Ann.

It was late night. Honey was in the shower. There was an e-mail. I opened it. And there it was in plain English.

When Honey came out of the bathroom, I was sitting on the edge of the bed.

"Have a seat," I told her.

She did. "What's up?"

"Ready?"

"Yeah."

"OK. I just got an e-mail from Carol Ann…."

"And…."

"And…the Evaline home and vineyard was sold last week for 1.6 million."

Her mouth slowly opened. Her head turned. She looked at the wall, the ceiling, the floor. She squinted. She bit her lip. Her robe opened slightly. For once in my life, I did not dive in, opening the robe more fully with my face. Instead, we just sat there."

I never thought to wonder who the buyers were.

Time passed. We never talked about Evaline. Honey seemed to want to believe that we were hoodwinked by a con man, paid to drive the price down, who got us drunk and had confederates downhill near the house. I wanted to believe that, too. But I couldn't. It didn't make sense. I knew what I had experienced.

Evaline was never far from my thoughts. The woman, the place, the story, the whole Evaline thing was my constant preoccupation. And because we never discussed it, I had no idea whether Honey was having the same experience, or if she had been able to move on. I knew that neither of us was the same.

About eight months after the Evaline place had sold, Honey spent a weekend in LA with her family. That Saturday morning, with no forethought whatsoever, I found myself driving north on the 101. I had no destination in mind. When I took the exit, I knew there was no chance I'd ever return to Evaline. Soon I found myself heading west out of Sebastopol, certain I could never turn onto that tiny road north. But I did. I felt like a helpless passenger as the car wound 'round the golden mountainside among the oaks. I was paralyzed in wonder as the car never slowed, crossing the valley and climbing the hill to the vineyard. It took me beneath the wooden arch and there, on the hillside, working in the vineyard, was Conrado.

"Ah…it's the dude," he said, smiling and shaking my hand.

"Still working here, huh?"

"Oh, si, still."

"Como esta?"

"Oh, muy bien. And how are you?"

"Good. Are the owners here?"

"Uh…si. They are here."

I was standing in almost the exact spot where I/Lawson stood that night/morning, yet the bad juju was strangely absent.

A woman came out of the house and walked up the trail toward us, just as Sarah/Evaline had. Probably in her fifties, she was striking, tall with warm brown eyes. I felt a wave of something. I think it was peace.

"Good morning," I said, introducing myself.

"Hello," she smiled, approaching me, extending her hand, "I'm Eve."

"Nice to meet you, Eve. Sorry if I'm intruding, I looked at this place months ago and it…made a big impression on me, so I just…just wanted to meet the new owners purely out of curiosity."

"That's no problem at all," she assured me with a glow, "You're welcome here."

"Thank you. Is your husband home?"

"Well...yes...," she told me with a look of confusion, "You're talking to him. This is my husband, Conrado. I thought you'd met."

"Oh.....uh......"

I turned and looked at Conrado, who smiled casually. I managed an "I see."

Then I looked back at her, into the gentle knowing of her eyes. "Eve," I tried to say, choking on the word.

"Yes."

The horizon was nowhere to be found. I was spinning, falling. Yet I was aware of my body standing there motionless, not even breathing. I knew. And suddenly I knew that I had known since that night. I knew what Lawson knew. That's what drew me back here. And I heard my voice say, "You're Evaline."

"Yes," she said, without surprise, "I am."

We stood there for several minutes after she went back to the house. Neither of us spoke. I was the one who finally broke the silence.

"You cheated me."

"I cheated no one."

"You drove the price down."

"That is true."

"I was going to buy this place."

"No one stopped you."

"You stopped me. You and your ghost, or whatever you did to me that night."

"The ghost is very real."

"Aw, c'mon...."

"You know this."

"You're a fraud. Did you show the ghost to others?"

"I did. Anyone was free to buy this house, this vineyard. But they would have to live with the ghost. There was nothing dishonest in introducing them."

"But you took advantage of…."

"I took advantage of no one. To live here the rest of my life, it is my destiny."

"Why?"

"You know why."

"I don't."

"You do."

I did.

"He knew."

"Yes."

"He never said anything."

"No."

"Why?"

"There was a time when Mr. McGee was an honorable man. He would never have done anything to disgrace my wife. Neither would Evaline. This is why she went so far away for so long."

"Why would she come back now?"

"This is our ghost to live with."

"I don't understand."

"You do. We have made this, my Eve and I, and it is we who must live here. It is our destiny now. So get your own ghost. I have no doubt that you will, dude. Life is like that."

There was nothing else to say. But still I didn't completely understand.

The front door opened, a typical college kid walked out and retrieved something from the car parked in front of the house. He was tall with dark skin. He waved, then went back inside.

And suddenly I understood.

I never told Honey. I didn't want to stir it all up again. She seemed to be putting the whole experience behind her.

I think about Conrado and Evaline often, about their destiny and their willingness to embrace it. After twenty years, they have found their happy ending. The cost is that they must live every day and night with the ghost of the man whose heart they betrayed, and the woman whose mind he betrayed because of it.

I never believed in ghosts. Now I know. I know what I have experienced. The sober-minded rational Capricorn in me has no answers, but he has a lot of questions. Did I become Lawson McGee that night? Or is that hatred and grief my own? Is there a difference? Why do I feel so guilty when I have done absolutely nothing wrong? Will Honey and I ever look at each other the way we once did? Will I ever again feel that I know myself and know Honey?

I have come to only one conclusion: that I am, at all times, surrounded by ghosts, not individual personalities, but vibrations of events that have lost their identity, yet retain their emotional energy. The acrid invasive juju is always by my side, and even closer, if I choose to notice. But while fear, grief and hatred release powerful vibrational energy, so do joy and ecstasy. Those ghosts surround me as well. They are as mysterious and indefinable as the fear-based ghosts, but also just as easily accessible, if one chooses to notice.

We finally found our dream house, a tiny ranch in Marin. No grapes. Horses.

Is it haunted? For years, when I have heard the phrase "holy water" I have quipped, "It's all holy." And now I have added a companion quip to that one. Whenever I hear mention of a "haunted house," I respond, "They're all haunted."

Maybe someday there will be another ghost in that vineyard, another ghost to join the fear and rage that haunt Evaline now. Another ghost that is two. A ghost of Love.

Months later, in our new home, the lights were off, I was already half-asleep, when a very pregnant Honey blurted, "Oh my God!"

She sat up and turned on the light, blinding me.

"What? What is it?" I moaned and winced.

"He was her lover!"

"What? Who...."

"Conrado was Evaline's lover! Think about it. Think about the things he said."

"I was almost asleep."

"I'm serious. Think about it. McGee didn't want them talking. He was jealous. She was very beautiful. All that stuff. Conrado was the reason she left. And he's still in love with her. Evaline."

How do women know these things? Someday I will have to ask Honey what she experienced that night in the vineyard. But I'm not ready for that ghost story yet.

TIRED EYES

Good night, Velma.
Shut your tired eyes.
The family is all here,
so smile one more time.
Good night, Velma,
I never knew you well,
but my father was your son,
and so I am your son as well.

Farewell, old gal…

Set your sails for the sun.
The day has come and gone.
Take your time as you go.
The twilights will guide you
home.

Good night, Mr. Elwood.
Put your Cadillac away,
and save all the short cuts
to be found another day.

Good day, tip your hat on your way.

Set your sails for the sun,
the day has come and gone.
Take your time as you go,
the twilights will guide you home.
Set your sails for the sun,
the day has come and gone.
The twilights will guide you on…

lyrics by Justin Tam

Goodnight Velma
Found Objects
2008
19.5 x 24 in
Julie Lee
Nashville, TN
www.julielee.org
julie@julielee.org.

SUNDAY SILHOUETTES

by Justin Tam

Memories inspired by the children of Bob and Velma Tam and their dear friend Martha Parker

The sharp right turn onto Main Street raises bumps on my skin. I haven't seen Elwood in over six years. My three siblings and I made the drive up from Indianapolis yesterday morning, enjoying a rare opportunity to be together again. We've kept a steady chatter going to distract from the purpose of our visit, but it still hangs heavy.

It's Sunday. Mother's ashes found their final resting place only yesterday afternoon, but it seems like ages ago as I witness spring along the small town roads. A colorful new life is sprouting in every flowerbed, providing an odd contrast to the black wardrobe the four of us exhibit. Stranger still, the grey interior of our rental vehicle matches my eldest sister's once brunette locks. At 58, I too have noticed my own follicles reflecting the same change. This return to our hometown has somehow cast light on the fading silhouette of my youth.

Familiar mid-western air floods refreshingly through our car windows, as I navigate at a slow thirty-five miles per hour. The downtown buildings of Elwood mirror my recollections but appear altered. We pass The White Spot, our first house on H Street and the drug store that now says Walgreens. The old Elks Club looks almost weary, its bronze statue covered with teal rust. J Street and K Street approach alphabetically.

Lost in the passing images, my pining is suddenly startled. A childish melody drifts audibly from the backseat,

"A, b, c, d, e, f, g…"

Hardly holding her tune, my giggling sister, three years my senior, is singing. I can't help myself: shaking my head with a grin, I chime in,

"…h, i, J!… K!… l, m, o, p…."

Chanting our "a, b, c's" was an Elementary school ritual. My sisters always managed to sing much faster than my younger memory could muster, but I relished the competition.

Our laughter subsides as we get closer to our destination. Three stoplights and two cornfields later we pull onto the street that taught us to drive. Like the prow of a ship pulling into port, our large hood ornament sails past a familiar white mailbox.

"9233 West Forest Drive," I jerk under my breath.

A smile in the rearview glass brightens, my 48-year-old younger brother knowingly reading my lips. The years have aged our brotherly bond into friendship. His ability to decipher my slightest expression is comforting today.

I place our car in park, and one by one each of us steps onto the freshly paved asphalt driveway. Our childhood house has been painted. It sold a few years back, after dad passed on and mom moved out to New Mexico. The trim is green now, but I miss the pink. The pink bathroom, the pink limestone, and pink formica countertops in the kitchen. I miss the walk-out basement with its sliding glass door. My mind still keeps mom's musty books on the ancient oak shelf—the one she built after taking a wood working class.

Staring at our former home, I find myself thinking how much quieter the weekly Sabbath has been these last five years. Before dad passed, I had an alarm. At six a.m. every Sunday morning that damn phone would ring, vibrating the nightstand. I'd roll over wearing a crinkled smile to pick up.

"What the hell are you doin' son?" he'd shout as if he had no idea I was two time zones behind his mid-western hide.

Sunday, phone lines eased the miles between us after I started my own family on the West Coast. No religious significance, Sunday was just the only day of the week dad couldn't work. The only day he took the time to reflect.

"If a dog hadn't stopped to take a shit in the woods he'd a caught the rabbit," he'd say chastising my over-sleeping.

He opened each phone call giving me a hard time, but really, he just wanted to hear his son's voice.

Dad was a well of these sort of laughable one-liners. As far back as I can recall, the passing of a graveyard would provoke dad's pointed elbow to nudge my side. With a smoker's voice he'd lean in, "Son, you know how many dead people are in that graveyard?"

He'd squish my knee until I couldn't take my own laughter and yell, "How many, dad?"

"All of 'em!! Ehhhh!!! Must be the dead center of town!"

We'd chuckle for a minute or two then he'd lean in again. We'd both say in chorus, "People are just dyin' to get in there!"

That would really send his whiskers rolling.

Dad orchestrated practical jokes as often as possible. As the friendliest person I've ever encountered, he definitely had plenty of candidates for his clowning. However, undoubtedly his closest friends and investment buddies, Chauncy Parker and Dr. Wally Scea, were my father's favorite targets.

After one particularly long night of brainstorming, as dad left Wally's house he noticed a stray goat oddly meandering in the street. Being the resourceful man that he was, my father quickly recalled the lengthy rope he kept handy in the trunk. He led the hungry goat back to a sleeping Dr. Scea's front lawn and tied it to a tree. By morning the very satisfied goat had consumed every blade of grass in sight. Dad denied the whole thing for weeks.

Despite his infamous tricks, everybody in town knew that Bob Tam was serious about business. He was an idea man, always workin' a new angle. Even on his deathbed, dad was closing a real estate deal with my sister's aid. As a small business owner, he ran a chain of Rexall Drugstores. Grandpa Merritt had helped dad buy into the company at an early age. Tam's Rexall were underfinanced and up against the "big boys." Only personal touch and local charm kept them afloat.

On Christmas Eve, dad's touch was keeping the Elwood corner store open late. I was ten years old when he first asked me to help and keep him company. Exhausted farmers and factory workers would shadow the brick doorway till midnight. With shallow pockets they'd purchase what they could for their families. One particularly chilly Christmas, a sun-wrinkled farmer approached me at the register. After five minutes of counting pennies, the man still needed twice the coin on the steel counter. My father approached softly, "Merry Christmas, friend… just pay when you can."

Working with dad was exhilarating. It was my first "job." I'd proudly man the chrome soda fountain and sneak caramel bits out of the Mason jar when my friends stopped in. I was too young to do much good, but it kept me away from my teasing sisters. Dad and I would pile into the big 225 Buick Electra and loudly hum down the dusty roads towards Anderson or Marion to check on the other drug stores. He'd sit me in his lap and let me steer, since I couldn't see over the dash, let alone reach the pedals. On my twelfth birthday, dad sat in the passenger seat and asked if I knew the way. His very trusting eyes closed for a quick nap, as I nervously navigated the one-lane gravel roads.

On our business trips, Dad liked to take alternate routes back to the house. He'd point out new tractors and poke fun at collapsing barns. We'd hold our noses pretending to puke passing a pungent chicken farm or dairy. Out of boredom or curiosity, dad would eagerly turn down almost any random road. A fun game most of the year, but the fully matured cornstalks of late summer created quite the maze for my trail-blazing father. Often, after an hour or so of keeping my loud mouth shut I'd have to inquire,

"…dad, are we lost?"

Gruffly he'd spit out the window, "Of course not! Just taking a short cut, son."

Three hours later we'd sheepishly roll onto this very driveway, lightning bugs flickering. I can see mom on the front stoop next to my sisters, cigarette in hand, shaking her red locks knowing what had happened.

She'd be proud of her front yard cherry trees today. Their trunks are enormous, their blossoms in bright bloom. "Must be worth a fortune in lumber," my brother says, proving genetics. Dad's entrepreneurial spirit would have said the same if mom hadn't planted their seeds with her own spade.

In our teenage days, friends and neighbors gathered under these front lawn cherry trees around the barbeque on many a warm Sunday afternoon. The heat never bothered my bottomless youthful stomach. Oh how I cringe now, noticing how my pillow-shaped gut has grown.

Compressing the dense grass with my brown leather loafers, I rest a lazy arm on sister's shoulder while I snap a few of dad's old jokes. The hearty chuckle from my mouth sounds more and more like dad's cackle, as we all pant with laughter. It feels rejuvenating to laugh so hard. It's hard to know what to feel these days... especially on a Sunday.

Not fifty yards from the garage the calm duck pond looks the same. To its left, the shiny metal flagpole is still proud. I'm not sure who raises its stripes each morning, but I'm grateful. Beyond it sits the golf course and its dated Country Club where we are headed for lunch.

It's only fitting. Our family ate there every Sunday. Astroturf green carpet still covers the floor of the 60's dining hall. The original colonial-style clubhouse burnt in the 1950's. Dad helped raise the funds for the modern building and later the sports bar where the four of us decide to order our meals. The country fried pork loin sandwich tastes like a heart attack to my healthy conscience, but I love it.

Eating out at the Country Club was a luxury in the town of Elwood. Most families couldn't afford it, but my mother Velma insisted. It was her day off. The rest of the week Mom's silky hands prepared our daily three square meals, putting up with my sister's picky complaints. A bell would jingle slightly before mom's voice called, "Get it now or starve later!"

Large portions of meat, baked potatoes, and a seasonal vegetable filled pastel plates at dinner. Slices of bacon coupled with scrambled eggs or fluffy pancakes graced the breakfast table. Dad's only duty was his hand crafted vanilla ice cream with nuts and maple syrup.

Velma, however, insisted on much more than a culinary day off. In fact, one late September afternoon, when my scream broke the peace of her aromatic kitchen, Velma's independence developed a need for transportation. Arriving at my panicked 5-year-old side, she quickly diagnosed a broken leg. With the family vehicle parked at the drug store, mom was stranded. She called the only cab in town and hoisted me into the back seat. The ER receptionist gave my apron-clad mother a hard time and the lazy doc took forever. The doc was very apologetic once he realized my father filled all his prescriptions, but it was too late. Velma's cheeks visibly matched her fiery hair by the time dad arrived.

The following morning Velma once again rang the lone cab driver, but this time I stayed behind. The cab dropped her off at the used car lot. That night when dad returned home, a large black Buick stood beaming in the driveway. Mom had taken out a loan in her own name and purchased a car without consulting my father. Dad was stunned.

Of course, Velma was used to defying convention. The car loan wasn't the first time she'd made a decision behind my father's back. While dad was away at war in the Pacific, mom won a raffle and purchased their first home, all while nursing my eldest sister. Indeed, it was this sort of gumption that had attracted my father to Velma. They met at Indiana University where mom received a bachelor's in business and a minor in journalism, quite the feat for a woman in the 1930's.

After college Velma took it upon herself to continue sharpening her mind. Piled each morning on the slate doorstep were the *Chicago Tribune*, the *Wall Street Journal*, the local *Cal Leader*, and several Indianapolis papers. Velma had an opinion on every issue and made it known. Elegant cocktail nights were a regular occurrence at our house. My eavesdropping little ears caught many political discussions drifting loudly from the living room, usually dominated by my mother.

Carefully stacked novels were a permanent fixture on mom's marble dresser. She'd finish three to five new titles per week. When I could stop my childish squirming long enough, I was allowed to sit next to my adolescent sisters while mom read us poetry and explained what it meant.

As I headed for bed each night, mom would be in the parlor recliner sipping coffee over an open book. Without fail, she'd wander to my bedside and tuck me in with a kiss. Her green pupils glowed against the red backdrop of my bedroom ceiling. She was my evening's end and security.

My parents' dimly lit doorway at the end of the hall dissolved the imaginary alligators I'd hurdle to reach the midnight bathroom. Often I'd make the long tiptoe to their bed and crawl in, dad's softly patterned snoring marching on. Mom wore a doily print nightgown with circles matching the yellow curlers locked in her hair. Her rose perfume calmed my kindergarten giggles. Snuggled under the puffy mauve comforter, we'd whisper with equal child-like voices.

"If you really try, little boy, you can do just about anything," she'd narrate.

"You can see the deserts of Africa… Egypt… and the ancient wonders! The sparkling stars are only as far away as you make them."

Thoughtfully she'd pause, seeming to believe her own words.

Letting out a sigh she'd say, "Ok now, Mr. Einstein. This day has come and gone. Another one tomorrow… go to sleep, tiny man."

I'd quiet down while the wispy song of her pages sang me to sleep, my tired eyes closing toward the grandest of places.

Mother's descriptions of faraway countries each night fueled her own desire to traverse the globe. Dad's penny-pinching style, however, didn't quite jive. So once we kids left home on our separate paths, Velma used an inheritance to join an organized group of like-minded vagabonds. She made her way eventually to Australia, New Zealand, Asia, and most of Europe.

When my folks did travel together, they'd vacation modestly with their best friends, Martha and Chauncy Parker. One year in the 1960's, dad uncharacteristically planned a Floridian excursion. We kids stayed behind with Grandma while the two Mid-Western couples headed south for the coast of northern Miami and found a beachfront motel.

The following morning Bob and Chauncy hastily set out fishing while the girls relaxed on the beach. Around noon, Velma received a message that the guys had ventured onto a boat and would be back by dark. No big deal. But when dusk fell a knock on the door delivered not Chauncy and Bob, but an urgent message from the eighty-mile off shore island of Bimini.

Velma,
It seems there's been a problem with the schooner. We might be gone a few days. Don't worry! Chauncy and I will be fine. Have fun at the motel!
— Bob

Not fooled for a minute, Velma was livid. The perturbed gals headed to the seedy motel bar and told everyone,"Our husbands have abandoned us and we're mad as hell!"

Velma turned to Martha resolutely and said, "Well, Martha, we're not going to sit around here all weekend are we?" Martha only curled a smirk.

By morning it was all arranged. The gals took a cheap cab to the airport and hopped on a flight to Bermuda! It was a tiny plane, and Martha and Velma made sure all the passengers knew the reason for their trip, even the pilot. When the wings passed over Bimini, the pilot tipped slightly to the right. Simultaneously, everyone thumbed their noses at the island as the gals waved victorious.

Chauncy and Dad arrived back at the seaside motel to an unexpectedly empty room. A note proudly resting on the pillow was inscribed,

> *Gone to Bermuda… be back soon, boys!*
> *— Love, Velma and Martha*

The guys thought it was a dumb prank until their first cocktail. The bartender confirmed the whole tale. The gals were "mad as hell" and had gone to Bermuda. Velma and Martha flew in the next morning, heads held high.

It must have been quite the amusing road trip back to Indiana. I can see them now, Bob and Velma with Chauncy and Martha in the family Cadillac. Big band music swingin' on the radio while the couples trade exaggerated stories.

That Cadillac is long gone now, but for a moment I recall its spaciousness as I climb into the backseat of our rental, my brother taking his turn behind the steering wheel. We have all repeated the nostalgic trek home to Indiana hundreds of times. Once more, we will retrace those well-trodden highways on our departure.

The sounds of our four automobile doors carry an unexpected weight knowing this may be the final time we return to Elwood. Home is not really here any longer. It too is becoming a silhouette, fainter the faster the years fly by. What we have of Elwood and our parents at this moment is all that we'll have for the rest of our lives.

"It feels good to reflect," I say, unintentionally aloud.

The rearview glass brightens once more, a confirmation from the front seat. It's the only thing *we* can do… It's Sunday.

"Quote" in Chicago, March, 2008

GRATITUDE

Record:

"quote" is forever grateful to the many musicians involved in this recording. Milis, an amazing traditional Irish duo—Niamh Varrian Barry on violin and vocals and Ilse De Ziah on cello. Caleb Mundy plays stand-up bass, and with the swing of his bow a percussion sample is born. Milis named him "Mr. Ears." Mike Odmark, a man of many instruments, playing on drums, dead skin of sacred albino elephant drum (again named by Milis), percussion, thumbtack piano, organ, and bass. Daniel Ellsworth on piano—so good. "Jazz Hands" Chris Farney on drums and percussion. Jamie Bennett on vocals, guitar, percussion, and glockenspiel. Justin Tam on vocals, guitar, percussion, and harmonica. No one can forget John Dupriest plucking his banjo. Finally, we thank Justin Carpenter and his trombone.

-Mike Odmark, we praise for six weeks of creative inspiration and a whole year of patience.
-Matt Odmark, we thank his mastering ears.

-Often overlooked, the quivers of equipment: Konrad, Josh Reynold, Justin "Boots" Herlocker, Jeff Gunckel, Dan Dehann, and Mike Odmark.

Literature:

-Jadyn Stevens for his love and devotion to this project, editing ideas and input, and patience. The chief editor, Maggie Monteverde, associate dean of the School of Humanities at Belmont University and much more—for her countless thankless hours spent bug-eyed in front of the computer screen looking over our mistakes, and for the tasty scones. Mike Stevens, his wife Priscilla, his son Jadyn, and the whole Eveready team, we love you guys. Thanks for a beautiful book. Matthew King for being a good friend and Frank Martino, the wonderful poet and true Sicilian. Sandy Craven, an eye for sarcasm, wit, and hope. Ashley Strosnider, whose rhythm gets our hearts jumping. Sean Edgehill for tolerance, and Motke Dapp, for understanding and simply good story telling. To Joel Fry, whose patience we also are indebted to, a wonderful poet at that. Kemper McDowell, for writing "the best ghost story I've read in a long time" (Maggie's husband Mike). Brandon Boyd, whose vigor and engaging story telling keeps his audience alive. Robin Gossard, Kent Tam, and Kevin Tam, children of Bob and Velma, thanks for all your work, memories, words, and wisdom. Martha Parker, for a tour of Elwood, good laughs and stories, and for lunch.

Art:
The Rymer Gallery – Tonya , Jeff and Herb, thanks for catching our vision.
Alissa Arnold for the recommendation. L.A Bachman, a good spirit and keen artist, one of our first Nashville friends. Kuntal Patel, for understanding so well our character. "All these years later and look what we did together." Casey Pierce, for a fantastic, new classic painting. Amanda Ball, thanks for the perfect pictures of two people meeting. John Whitten, whose sketches reveal so much depth. Sara La, for being ever so prompt, hard working, and so talented. Myles Bennett, for the brilliant approach you've created in your Bushwick Flat. Julie Lee, for your family instincts and lovely touch. J.K. Lee for her understanding. James De Boer for a long time friendship and a brilliant depiction. Also thanks to Bennett Galleries Nashville for the stretch. To Candy Pyburn from Wondergraphics, for wonderful prints.

Additional Thanks:
Joyce Oberle for her ability to believe in our vision. Rebecca Bennett, a brilliant flutist. Fred Bennett, for his participation in WW2, his stories, humor, and good memory. To Margaret Profita, for your thoughts about the war, your wisdom, and love. All of our wonderful supporting family. We love you all!!! Eric Wilkey, for his skills in photography and culinary genius. Chris Plank for his photography. Evan Goodberry for putting up with our noise and messes. Mike, coffee and cigarettes. Father Odmark, for the use of your instrument. Valerie Hammond, countless flyers and graphical talents. Emily Keafer, additional design and last minute brilliant work. Lance, for teaching us to sing. Cotton Music, for running the acoustic guitar mecca. Bonsall, Sullivan Middle School, and fate for planting the seed for "quote." Riverview. The ocean. Wind. The metaphysical mysteries (God)...and Love

www.quotemusic.net

www.myspace.com/quotemusic